EROTIC QUICKIES

A TOUCHSTONE BOOK
PUBLISHED BY SIMON & SCHUSTER
NEW YORK   LONDON   TORONTO   SYDNEY

Heidi's Bedtime Stories

for MEN & WOMEN

Heidi Cortez

 TOUCHSTONE
Rockefeller Center
1230 Avenue of the Americas
New York, NY 10020

TOUCHSTONE and colophon are registered trademarks
of Simon & Schuster, Inc.

For information regarding special discounts for bulk purchases,
please contact Simon & Schuster Special Sales at
1-800-456-6798 or business@simonandschuster.com.

Designed by Jan Pisciotta

Manufactured in the United States of America

10   9   8   7   6   5   4   3   2   1

ISBN-13: 978-0-7432-9804-9
ISBN-10:   0-7432-9804-7

To my friend Howard,
thanks for more than just the inspiration . . .
I f'ing love you!

Introduction

I love to watch couples. Doesn't matter where. I might see them in a crowd at a ball game or standing in line at the post office, and I'll start to imagine how they might have met or what type of experiences they've had with each other. That's where the stories in this book come from: my imagination. And, as you'll see, my imagination sometimes runs wild.

When I was nineteen I made an audio CD of erotic stories called *Sexxxy Noises*. I told short, three- to seven-minute stories, drawing on what I imagine people might do together. I lay there on the recording studio floor by myself with my eyes shut, headphones on, and the mic close to my mouth. I have a nervous habit of stroking my inner thighs while telling my stories, but I guess it puts me in the right mood. I thought about the people I might have seen earlier in the day or week, about what their sensual stories might be. I love to see

people in love, or falling in love, or just turned on by each other. Then I created a story around them.

The CD was a big hit. Soon everyone was asking for more stories, and great things started happening for me. Being a fan of *The Howard Stern Show* since I was twelve years old, I sent him *Sexxxy Noises,* hoping he would get a kick out of it. Well, he did. He played my CD weekly for about two years. When we finally met, we hit it off and I developed a good relationship with the Stern family. Two years later, the king of all media asked me to host his new creative radio show called *Tissue Time with Heidi Cortez.* I was, of course, thrilled. I love being in the recording studio, and telling these stories is another way I can express myself. That awesome opportunity started me on a new career, and soon after I was approached by the wonderful crew at Simon & Schuster to put my wild imagination onto paper. That became *Heidi's Bedtime Stories.* Here you'll find extraordinary encounters in the most ordinary places—a laundry room, a chiropractor's office, a beach picnic, even in a shoe store.

Recording *Sexxxy Noises;* my radio show, *Tissue Time*

with Heidi Cortez; and writing *Heidi's Bedtime Stories* has been the most fun I've ever had. I hope in reading my bedtime stories you'll become inspired and unleash your imagination . . . just a tad more.

Heidi Cortez

I live in a small town, so when I visited New York City for the first time, I was just in awe. From the moment I arrived at JFK, everything seemed to be moving at top speed. Even the superfast taxi ride to Manhattan was exciting and scary. When I got to the hotel in Times Square, I was almost overwhelmed by the glittering lights and the people rushing around. I felt so small surrounded by all the towering buildings and huge billboards. The hotel lobby was gorgeous with its marble floors, ornate chandeliers, and glass-enclosed elevators. Since I didn't know anyone in New York I spent a lot of time in my room. Sure it got boring, but I was waiting to meet my boyfriend, who wouldn't arrive for another few days. We live in different cities and hadn't seen each other for two months. We'd

agreed to meet in New York. It would be the first visit for us both.

One particular night will always remind me of New York. It started off pretty normally. I was sitting on the bed in front of the floor-to-ceiling windows, with a glass of wine at my side, taking in the beautiful city from my twenty-second-floor room. From up so high the city was spread out like a shimmering tapestry before me. I could make out at least two bridges in the distance and the lights of the cars glittered below in red and green. At night with their lights on it was easy to see inside other buildings.

The past two nights I'd taken to looking into the same apartment where this good-looking guy lived. With his dark hair and sexy beard, he reminded me of my boyfriend. He'd come in, turn on the lights, take off his work shirt, sit down on the couch, and turn on the television. Even from far away I could tell he had a great body. He had a muscular chest and a well-defined six-pack. He had the sexiest arms I've ever seen, and his worn jeans, which hung low on his hips, showed off his tight ass. I figured he worked with his body because he was in great shape.

That night, instead of just watching TV and falling asleep, he sat on his sofa stroking his chest with his fingers. I couldn't really tell, but I think he was watching porn. I started getting turned on as he ran his fingers across his nipples and then between his legs, roughly rubbing his dick. He looked so hot, I was getting really horny. I started rubbing my shoulders and caressing my breasts. When I felt my pussy getting wet, I slid my hand inside my panties. I pretended it was my boyfriend's fingers between my legs as I stroked myself.

I felt like a Peeping Tom as I sat there in my short silk robe watching this good-looking stranger touch himself. When he unzipped his jeans, pulled out his swollen cock, and started stroking it, I slid out of my robe and let it fall to the floor. It was so hot watching him without his knowing it. I could feel how wet my pussy was getting, and I badly wanted to come. I lay down facing the window with my legs up on the bed. I started caressing my inner thighs, slowly teasing myself as I got closer to my throbbing clit. I was going crazy. It felt sooo good. I licked my fingers and slowly ran them down my body all the way to my clit.

My pussy was soaked, and I loved it. I slipped my

fingers between my swollen lips and rubbed the juice all over. I still had plenty left to smear over my breasts to make my nipples hard. I was so close to coming. The faster the stranger stroked his dick, the harder I rubbed my clit. My pussy was throbbing, and I wished I had my boyfriend's fat cock to fill me up right then and there. I could feel the muscles in my body tighten as I fingered myself.

I was so close; my juices were running down my legs. I was moaning louder and louder. My whole body tensed up as I watched my stranger stiffen and come in his hand. I couldn't hold it anymore; it was getting really intense, and my moans were getting louder, my mouth was getting dry. And then there . . . "Oh, fuck!" I screamed so loud, my own body jerking on the bed now soaked with my cum. I moaned loudly and gasped for air until I lay back limp, my arms at my side. I felt so much better. I wished I could thank my good-looking stranger. Maybe I'd see him tomorrow.

My best friend, Julie, wanted me to go on a blind date with this guy David, whom she knows from work. Blind dates aren't my thing, but after about a week of her begging, I gave in and told Julie he could call me.

David called that Friday. He sounded nice enough and had a deep sexy voice. We talked for a bit, getting to know each other. He mentioned that he has a buddy with a great place in Malibu. When he asked if I'd like to go to his friend's beach party, I said yes, partly to make Julie happy and partly because I wanted to meet him. He arranged to pick me up at eight that night. I hung up the phone with a smile and a warm tingling between my legs.

I'm a big sucker for the ocean, and a Malibu beach party sounded like fun. I wanted to look smoking hot that night.

Who knew who was going to be there! Plus, I wanted to impress David.

I went shopping and found this beautiful chocolate brown cotton dress. It was short and tight, and showed off my long tanned legs. The high slits on either side would be perfect over my bikini. When I slipped it on in the dressing room, I looked great. The color complemented my bronzed skin and my long blonde hair. David was in for a treat.

That evening I stepped out of the shower and stood naked in front of the mirror admiring my long legs, small waist, and full breasts. I pulled out my ponytail and let my long hair fall down my back. I then slipped on my white bikini and my high-heeled sandals. My stomach was flat, and my ass was toned from hours at the gym. I smiled at my reflection, and after slipping on my little summer dress I was ready.

When I opened the door to let David in, I almost gasped. He was *hot!* Julie hadn't told me he used to be a model. In his tight jeans and T-shirt I could tell that he had a great body. He was about six feet two inches, 190 pounds, with sexy teal-colored eyes and thick salt-and-pepper hair. When he smiled, he had deep dimples and

even white teeth. I'm only twenty-four and not normally into older men, but the moment I saw David I could feel my pussy getting wet.

After a couple cocktails at my place, we hopped into his Jeep and headed to Malibu. It was a gorgeous evening, and the fresh sea air made me feel alive and happy. We arrived at the party a little late. Everyone was already wasted and making their way down to the ocean. As we walked around the house, we came across the hot tub, which was empty. I begged David to get in with me, but he didn't have his trunks. I led him to the bar, and many shots of Patron Silver later he was ready to take the plunge.

We walked to the hot tub, and I smiled at David as I stepped out of my dress, standing there in my bikini and heels. I could see his dick getting hard. I stepped close to him and slid my hand into the front of his pants. David's breathing deepened, and his dick grew thicker. The more excited he got, the wetter my pussy became. I was looking forward to getting him naked and in the hot tub.

I undid his vintage jeans and pulled them down to his ankles and he stepped out of them. He had strong

thighs and calves, just the way I liked them. He wasn't wearing any underwear, and he had a nice big dick. Then I pulled his T-shirt over his head. His chest was almost completely hairless and well muscled, and he had a firm flat stomach. Using his shoulder for support, I kicked off my sandals and stepped into the hot tub. Then I sat down and waited for David to join me.

With a big smile David stepped into the hot tub and came toward me. I pulled him closer and started kissing him. He held me by my shoulders and kissed my neck, then he pulled my legs around his waist as I straddled his lap. I could feel his hard dick through my bikini bottom. I started rocking my hips back and forth over his naked cock and sucking lightly on his neck. David moaned, and I felt his hand go up my bikini top. He fondled my tits, making my nipples hard. I gasped when he sucked one deep into his mouth. It felt so good when he slipped his hand into my bikini and shoved his two thickest fingers up my twat. I moaned even louder as he roughly finger-fucked me, stroking my clit and burying his face in my big breasts as he sucked on my nipples.

I was happy to return the favor and started stroking

his thick cock. I slid out of my bikini bottom and rubbed his dick on my slick clit. I couldn't believe what we were doing. I was getting more and more turned on, my moans getting louder as I felt myself about to come. David stood up and sat me on the edge of the hot tub. He then positioned his dick between my legs, grabbed my ass, and shoved deep inside me. I moaned with pleasure as my body trembled, and I came hard all over his slippery cock. David then started fucking me hard. One hand at my waist and the other on my shoulder, he bounced me up and down on his cock until he pulled out and shot his cum between my breasts. What a great date. I couldn't wait to thank Julie for hooking us up. I thought we clicked quite well.

My friend Claire and I have known each other since the seventh grade. We share almost everything together: clothes, homework, and sometimes boyfriends. Claire is gorgeous. She has curly dark hair, green eyes, and freckles that she hates but that are really cute. Her long tanned legs, small waist, and big breasts always get her plenty of attention. When we go out together, we get jealous stares from just about every woman we pass. But we're used to it, and we love it!

"It's Saturday night, and I want to go out," Claire said with a huge grin on her face. I knew what that meant. She wanted to get wasted and fuck the first hot thing she saw. Since neither one of us is even close to being twenty-one, we usually dated older guys. That way we can get drinks. I met

this guy, Steve, on the Internet about two weeks ago and had mentioned him to Claire a few times. She suggested that we call him. From his picture he was pretty good-looking, and since he was thirty-four, I knew he'd be able to get us into a club. I called him.

Before we hooked up with Steve, Claire and I put on our "slut gear" so we'd look older. I was wearing super-low-rise jeans that made my ass look perfect. My sequined top was short and tight, and my titties hung out just a little when I bent over. Claire borrowed my pink tank top and matching little pink skirt, which made her long legs look like she was a supermodel. Every time she sat down, I had to tell her to cross her legs because she wasn't wearing panties. She'd just giggle. She thinks it's funny that she doesn't like panties.

We met up with Steve, who was just as good-looking in person. He took us to dinner and then later to Club Joe's, the most happening club anywhere on a Saturday night. Steve didn't know that Claire and I weren't yet twenty-one. I told him that I'd lost my ID the night before at another bar. Being such a sweet guy, he got us in. I headed to the bar to get drinks, and when I turned

around, Claire was freak dancing with Steve. I couldn't wait to get out there and join them.

The later it got, the drunker we got, the more we danced and the sweatier we were. I was getting so turned on looking at Steve, wondering what that bulge in his pants might look like. I started rubbing my pussy slowly against his thigh. With a drunken smile I pulled Claire toward us. She held my waist and then started to lick my collarbone. Oh, my God, it was the sexiest thing. I reached inside the waistband of Claire's skirt from behind and slid two fingers into her tight little twat. It was easy since she wasn't wearing any panties.

I wanted to please Steve and her at the same time, so I turned around and started rubbing my ass on Steve's crotch as Claire and I kissed. She stuck her soft tongue deep inside my mouth and slid her hand between my legs. My pussy was dripping, soaking my jeans. She fingered my clit, outlined by my tight jeans. It felt so good. All I wanted to do was go somewhere private and rip all our clothes off. I turned around and asked Steve to pay for a VIP room where the three of us could be alone.

The second we got upstairs to the VIP room, the

three of us just went crazy. I started kissing Claire while reaching over to unbuckle Steve's pants. Being only eighteen, I had never seen or felt a dick so big. My mouth was watering. I pulled off my top so he could play with my tits and dropped to my knees to suck him off. As I slid his huge cock in my mouth, Claire got down on her knees behind me and pulled down my jeans and wet panties. I felt her mouth on my pussy as she sucked hard on my cunt. Whenever she'd lick my clit, my body would tremble.

Steve grabbed the back of my head and forced his cock deep into my mouth. I started choking and could barely breathe. Every time I tried to pull away he would hold my head tighter, forcing me to suck harder. My mouth was aching, but what Claire was doing to my throbbing pussy made everything okay. The more they both took advantage of me, the more turned on I got.

Steve pulled his dick out of my mouth and bent us both over the sofa. Claire and I started kissing each other hungrily as Steve pulled my jeans all the way down, then pushed Claire's skirt over her ass. He then took turns fucking our tight little pussies from behind. I'd never been this turned on. Steve grabbed my hips

and fucked me harder until I started to come, my juices coating his dick. He then pulled out and started fucking Claire. Claire was moaning so much it was hard for us to keep kissing. I knew she was close to coming. I stopped kissing her to watch my good friend come. As Steve rammed his dick into her, she screamed loudly, her body shaking as Steve pulled his cock out of Claire and came all over my tits.

Our wonderful night came too quickly to an end. I couldn't believe the things we'd done. That night Claire and I promised each other that we'd never tell anyone what happened. And we never did. Today we're still best friends and enjoy each other when our parents aren't around.

Dear Diary:

I'm not sure if I should be confessing to you or to Father Joe, but last night I lost my virginity. I wasn't planning on it. It just sort've happened.

After dinner with Dad, I went upstairs, put on my PJs, and got into bed. I was sleeping when it felt like I was having one of those wet dreams again. But it was a different feeling last night. It felt especially good. As I lay there with my eyes closed I felt a hand on my inner thigh. I opened my eyes but saw nothing; figuring I'd been dreaming, I went back to sleep. A few moments later, I felt a hand on my body again. I sat up and saw a shadow in my room. I was scared. Then a man said my name and told me he thought I was beautiful. He said he'd been watching me for

years. I must know him, I thought. Maybe he wasn't a stranger, I thought . . .

He came over to the bed, but, with the curtains drawn, I still couldn't see his face. He started touching me softly in places I'd never been touched before. I knew I should tell him to stop, but it felt too good. He pulled me to the edge of the bed, knelt down on the floor, and pulled my panties off. He then licked his finger and slid it into my ass as he put his mouth on my pussy. I started to resist, but he started to get rough with me. I tried not to make much noise. I would have died of embarrassment if my parents had walked in.

He got on the bed and held both my wrists above my head, pinning me down. Then he forced his heavy body onto mine. He pulled out his penis and started to rub it up and down my clit, and started sucking hard on my nipples as he reached around and fondled my body with his other hand.

As he sucked and licked my body he kept saying I was dirty and he was just trying to help. He then turned me over, shoved my head in the pillow, pulled my hips up off the bed, and shoved his penis deep in me. It hurt so much but in a good way. He moaned loudly as he

fucked me harder and harder. My pussy was hurting so bad. He grabbed my shoulders tight and pounded his hips against mine, then groaned loudly. After a few moments he pulled out and told me to keep my eyes closed. I heard him leaving through the window. After a few more minutes I opened my eyes. I was alone.

Diary, I feel really ashamed now. I didn't mean for it to happen. Please forgive me.

I live in my apartment with my roommate, Tina. Every week, on Thursday night, we take turns doing laundry in the laundry room. We both hate doing laundry, and we always bicker about whose turn it is. Since I was going out tomorrow night, I knew that if I wanted my favorite pair of low-rider jeans to be clean, I'd have to wash them myself. I gathered the laundry, my iPod, and my massive pile of homework and headed downstairs. Nobody's *ever* there at eleven P.M., so I left the apartment wearing pink boy shorts and a wife beater.

I started my first load and figured I might as well wash what I was wearing. If I didn't, who knew when I'd get around to it? I slipped out of the shorts and top and threw them into the washing machine. Then I sat down in the cor-

ner of the laundry room, put my headphones on, turned on my iPod, and started doing my homework. There's nothing like a little Beastie Boys while doing the laundry.

Every so often I'd pull my headphones to the side to hear if the washing machine had stopped. About a half an hour into doing my laundry, I looked up and my heart about stopped: my boyfriend, Kevin, was standing in the doorway smiling at me!

I pulled off my headset and yelled at him for scaring me. He said he hadn't meant to, but he thought it was very sexy that I was in the laundry room in only my panties. He asked me if I could go back to what I was doing and pretend he wasn't there. I'd never done anything like that before, but it sounded kinky and I agreed. I put my headphones back on and looked down at my book, waiting for Kevin to say or do something. When I looked up, he was standing by the light switch. He smiled at me and then flipped off the switch.

With only a little light from the street shining in I could barely see him. My heart started racing. I was a little scared, but I knew I was safe with him. A moment later I felt Kevin between my legs on his knees. He

pulled my panties down to my ankles and pulled me to the edge of the chair. He then started licking and kissing my inner thighs, closer and closer to my clit. It was complete torture! It felt so good; every time he licked close to my clit I'd start to come. I so badly wanted him to put his mouth on it. He then slid his hand below my ass, slipped his thumb into my tight little pussy and his index finger up my ass, and started to slide them both in and out. Mmm, it felt so good. I was completely soaking the chair. After a few minutes he pulled his fingers out and, with a big smile, sucked my juice off his thumb.

Kevin then picked me up and laid me down on one of the folding tables. He roughly pushed back my knees toward my head and pulled my ass closer to the edge. He gave my pussy a long deep kiss as he pulled down his pants. I don't remember his cock ever feeling so big and hard. It was only a matter of seconds before he'd shoved his cock deep inside me. Kevin started pounding my twat so hard I thought the table would break. He reached behind me grabbed a fistful of my long blond hair and yanked it until I was almost in tears. I could feel the head of his dick deep inside me. My cum was

running down my ass, making the table slick. As I got closer to coming, he licked two fingers and rubbed them up and down my clit as he fucked me harder. I screamed out as I came all over Kevin's cock.

To this day Kevin and I love doing laundry on Thursday nights. . . .

When I was a little girl, my dad would take my sister and me to the Los Angeles Dodgers baseball games. I was fascinated with baseball and thought it was the best thing ever. Although I'm older, I still appreciate the sport, but now I find myself liking it for a different reason: the players! I can't help it. I love watching those hot men act like boys as they run around in their tight pants. Mmm. It makes my pussy twitch just thinking about it.

Last Sunday, I caught a game with my friend Cassie. As far as I'm concerned all the players are hot, but my favorite player, Jason Howard, is tall, tanned, and has eyes so blue you can see them from across the field. I've had a crush on him for at least two seasons. And I've been wearing sexy little outfits

to the games, trying to get his attention for almost as long. Today I was a wearing a fringed, denim miniskirt, a white tank top that made my big breasts look even bigger, and strappy tan sandals. I love showing off my long legs, which people tell me are my best features.

After the game I saw Cassie talking to my hottie by the restrooms. I got so jealous that I ran over and introduced myself. "Hi, Jason, I'm Pearl. I'm a *huge* fan," I gushed, flirting with my big brown eyes. I saw Cassie smile as she said good-bye, then walked away. I couldn't believe I had my dream man in front of me. Before I lost my nerve I asked Jason if he wouldn't mind taking me on a small tour of the dugout. I explained to him how my father would take me here when I was little and that I've always dreamed of seeing the dugout. Jason smiled and said, "I'd be happy to give you a tour, little lady. But it'll have to be a short one. I'm pretty dirty and sweaty, and I'd like to take a shower."

As I followed him into the dugout my heart was beating so fast I thought he could hear it.

"Well, this is it, Pearl. The dugout you've wanted to see for so many years. I hope you're not disappointed," he said with a soft laugh.

I couldn't have cared less about the dugout. What I really wanted was for Jason to shove me up against the cement wall and rip my clothes off. I haven't had sex in six months and I was so horny I was about to do the unthinkable. I saw a bucket of used baseballs in a corner. I walked over to them and ever so slowly bent to pick one up. I knew my little denim skirt was barely covering my ass as I reached down for a baseball. I could feel his piercing blue eyes as I said innocently, "May I have this? It would be a great souvenir."

Jason laughed and said, "Pearl, do you always get what you want?"

I smiled and said in my sexiest voice, "Sometimes, but not always." I then sat down on the bench with my legs slightly apart. I knew that Jason would see that I wasn't wearing any panties. He stood there and tried to talk to me for a few minutes, but I noticed he kept sneaking peaks at my pussy. I put my hand on my leg and started casually rubbing my thigh. When he sat on the bench next to me, I placed his hand on my leg and told him to feel my goose bumps. Jason smiled and said, "You shouldn't wear so little when it's still a bit chilly out."

He then started rubbing my legs to warm me up. Every few rubs he would get closer and closer to my pussy. I wanted him to slide his thick fingers inside me so badly. I put my hand over his and slid it up my skirt between my legs as I opened my legs wider. "Mmm," I moaned, leaning back against the wall. I knew Jason was getting excited. I could see how hard his dick was through his tight uniform. I took his other hand and put it on my breast. My nipples were so hard. He grabbed my breast tightly, put his mouth on my nipple, and started sucking hard. I moaned loudly, getting more turned on. I wanted to please him so badly, I pulled my breast out of his mouth and got on my knees between his legs.

The stadium was pretty much empty now, and it was pretty dark in the dugout. But I could still see what I was doing. I pulled his pants down around his ankles and stroked his enormously hard cock. I looked Jason in his gorgeous blue eyes as I rubbed the head of his cock on my lips. It felt so good on my mouth. I softly licked the head, flicking my tongue across the tip. He tasted so good. I must have been driving Jason crazy because he groaned and then yanked back my head and

shoved his dick deep into my throat. I could barely breathe. He kept shoving my head up and down until I was almost choking on his cock. Gripping my long hair, he pulled my mouth off his dick, then groaned, "Stand up." When I stood, he said, "Straddle my cock." I was more than happy to do it. I hiked up my miniskirt, positioned his dick at my twat, and straddled his cock like he asked. My pussy was hot and throbbing. I slowly sat on his dick, moving my hips back and forth so I could feel him deep inside me.

He pulled my top over my breasts and drew me closer so he could put his face between my bouncing titties. His large hands were on my hips, and I got the feeling it was no longer about me. He gripped so hard and tight that I knew I was going to have bruises, but I didn't care. He closed his eyes and fucked my pussy so hard I was almost in tears. Jason groaned, "I'm gonna come deep in you."

"Oh, yeah, fuck me like that," I moaned.

Then he yelled out, "Ohhh, fuck!" He had come, and I was dying to come, too.

He pulled out, picked me up, and sat me on the bench with my legs spread open. He then started kiss-

ing me and stroking my clit, slipping a thick finger inside me with every stroke. I was only seconds from the strongest orgasm I had ever had. "Oh," I groaned. And then I came so fucking hard I could feel my cum run down my thighs.

Later, I apologized to Jason for keeping him from his shower. He laughed and said, "Anytime." We then exchanged numbers and promised that we'd keep in touch. But honestly, it doesn't matter if I ever see him again. What happened that night was a dream come true and it is what it is.

It was my twenty-fifth birthday and my two best girls, Kerry and Robin, were taking me out. I'd been looking forward to this night for weeks. I live in New York, but most of my friends live in Jersey, where I'm from. We don't get to see one another that often, so I was expecting tonight to be pretty special.

Since it was my birthday I decided the more daring the clothes, the better. I wore my dark hair out in loose spiral curls. My jeans were tight and very low on my hips. My tight knit top was black with a large V cut in the front and backless to my waist. I then slid my feet into a sexy pair of silver heels. By ten P.M., I was all dolled up and ready to paint the town rainbow when my doorbell rang. "Jess! Are you ready?" Kerry yelled into the intercom. "Yes," I answered as I grabbed my handbag and headed out the door.

"So, ladies, what's the plan?" I asked eagerly when we were all in the cab. They giggled and said I'd just have to wait. I was really curious now, but I didn't say anything. I knew they'd take good care of me. First we stopped at this bar called Smokey's. It was filled with good-looking people, and hot guys were buying me shots for at least an hour because it was my birthday. We were all getting pretty buzzed and having a great time. I figured the plan was that we'd hit another spot and then all crash at my place since I lived in the city. Around eleven-thirty Robin said it was time for my big surprise and that we had to get going if I wanted my present while it was still my birthday. I laughed, and we got into another cab.

Robin handed the cabdriver directions to our destination. I was so buzzed that I didn't really care where we were going. Kerry pulled a black silk handkerchief out of her purse and told me to close my eyes. When I did, she blindfolded me and said not to take it off until she told me to. About ten minutes later the cab stopped and they helped me out. I heard loud music and voices. I figured we were at a club. "Can I please open my eyes?" I begged. I was beginning to think it was pretty immature that I couldn't open my eyes.

Robin laughed, "Just a little longer." She told me to sit down. "Wait a few minutes, and I'll be right back." I heard them giggling around me and started to wonder what was going on. Why couldn't I open my eyes? Why was it so loud? And why was my head spinning?

Next thing I knew Robin whispered in my ear that she had a friend, Jasmine, with her. She said that Jasmine was going to take me someplace quiet, where we would be alone, and that I should do whatever she said. Jasmine guided me by the hand into a quiet room that seemed a short distance away and sat me down. "Are we still in public?" I asked nervously, wondering who this Jasmine was. Then she untied the handkerchief and said I would be able to open my eyes when she said it was okay. I laughed. "What is this, a strip club?" I asked. I heard music start playing, and Jasmine said, "Open your eyes." When I did, I was staring right at the V between her legs. Her pussy was so close I could smell her scent. I was in shock, but I didn't want her to stop.

She was beautiful with long dark brown hair and deep blue eyes. She had a dancer's body and was wearing a cute little outfit. Her sheer pink short skirt just skimmed her ass, and her matching pink bra top barely

covered her big tits. She was tall and had a perfect body. Even her stilettos were sexy.

Jasmine started dancing in front of me, pushing her tits in my face and grinding her hips into mine. She turned around, bent over, grabbed an ankle with one hand, then used the other hand to stroke her pussy. I couldn't believe how turned on I was getting. "Do you like girls?" Jasmine asked with a sexy smile. I told her that this was my first time even thinking about it. She smiled again, then turned around and straddled my knees, rubbing her clit on my leg. Her panties were so thin I could tell she was shaved. She sat on my lap and licked between my breasts down into the V neck of my top, then she took one of my nipples in her mouth and sucked hard on it. My pussy got so wet I knew I was soaking my jeans.

Jasmine sucked one nipple, then the other. When she was done, she put her arms around my neck, brought her perfect breasts up to my face, and whispered, "Suck my nipples." I couldn't believe what was happening, but I figured, what the hell. I probably won't even remember it in the morning. The whole point of tonight was to be daring and have a good time. And I was definitely having a good time! As she rubbed her big soft breasts over my lips I

started sucking on them, moving from one nipple to the other. I licked and then sucked them into my mouth as Jasmine moaned and ground her pussy into my crotch.

She then opened the zipper of my jeans and slipped her hand between my legs. It felt so good to have Jasmine touch my pussy. I was so horny I wished she'd finger-fuck me. When she rubbed her nipples against my mouth, I sucked hard on them. "Yes, just like that," Jasmine moaned softly. The more turned on she got, the more I did, too. I needed to come.

I sucked on her nipples as she rubbed her almost naked body against me. She slid her fingers deeper inside me and finally started to finger-fuck me until my pussy was dripping wet and quivering. "Mmm . . ." I moaned, sucking hard on her tits. I was too embarrassed to tell her I was coming. But she was a professional, and I'm sure she knew. After I came Jasmine slipped her tits out of my mouth and squeezed them together with her hands. Then, as she fingered her nipples with one hand, she rubbed my fingers hard on her pussy with her other hand until I felt her come.

The next morning when I was sober I made sure to share my experience with my friends and to thank them.

I love shoes. Nothing's sexier than a pair of four-inch heels with sexy jeans or a hot dress.

It had been a while since my last shoe fix, so I stopped by this great store on Ocean Drive to get some killer heels. Something along the lines of strappy metallic sandals, to go with my black lace cocktail dress.

It was late in the day, and the store was empty. I was able to browse at my leisure without worrying that someone might get the last pair I wanted. Then I saw them, exactly what I wanted, four-inch-high gold sandals that laced halfway up the calf. I could barely contain myself.

When I took them off the stand, the tall young salesclerk asked me if I needed help. His name tag said DANNY, and he seemed nice enough, attentive but not pushy. He looked a

little like a science geek, but behind his wire frames he had sexy hazel eyes. And his thick brown hair was boyishly tousled. His baggy jeans and button-down shirt hid a muscular body. I could always tell. I smiled and asked him to please bring me a size seven. When he disappeared into the back room, I kept my fingers crossed, hoping he'd come back with my size and color. (Ladies . . . you know what I'm talking about.)

When he came out with a box and a big smile, I knew he'd found them for me. I was so excited to see if they fit that I almost snatched them out of his hand. I couldn't wait to try them on.

"Oh, these are so cute," I said as I took the gorgeous shoes out of the box and sat down to try them on.

"Please, let me," Danny said as he took the shoes from my hand and laid them on the seat next to me. He then knelt down between my legs and lifted one of my feet.

I forgot that in some shoe stores they'll place your foot in the shoe for you, to make sure that you don't damage them. But I didn't think Danny was worried about my damaging the shoes. In fact, he was really taking his time with me. He *very* slowly placed one foot

then the other on his knees, slid them out of my pumps, and exposed my newly pedicured feet. I have a thing about my feet. I like them to be smooth and to have my toenails always painted. I knew they felt soft in Danny's hands.

Danny smiled as he slid off each pump. Then he started rubbing my toes and the balls of my feet. It felt so good I didn't say anything, but it sure felt weird to get a foot massage in a shoe store. He then carefully slid one foot into a sandal. He placed my sandaled foot against his knee as he wound the laces around my calf. He then gently placed that foot on the ground and did the same thing with my other foot.

When he was done, he said, "You sure have beautiful feet. They're the perfect size, and your toes are gorgeous."

I didn't know what to say, so I just laughed.

"How do you like those?" he asked. "They sure look great on you."

I lifted up one foot and took a long look. He was right; they looked great. They'd look even better with my lace dress.

I was really happy with my find, but I was even more

excited by Danny. It was clear to see that he had a foot thing. It made sense; he worked in a woman's shoe store. I liked the way he'd caressed and massaged my feet, so I thought I'd give him a little thrill.

I lifted up the other foot in the sandal and turned my leg one way and then the other. "What do you think? Do these make my feet look good?" I asked innocently.

Danny became agitated; there were beads of sweat on his upper lip. He even stammered a little when he answered, "Of course . . . um, yes, yes, very beautiful." He smiled shyly. "You have the most beautiful feet I've ever seen."

I stretched one leg up onto the seat across from me and admired my foot in the sexy sandal.

"Do you think I need to wear panty hose with these?" I asked as I pulled up my sundress a little to show off my firm thighs.

"Absolutely not," he answered, never taking his eyes off my feet.

I was starting to have fun, and Danny was kinda cute. He was in for a treat. "I think I'll take them," I said. "Would you mind undoing the straps for me?"

Danny looked at me with such joy that I knew I'd

made his day, maybe his month. "It would be a plea-sure," he said. He sat up on the chair opposite me, faced me, and placed my leg on his knee. Slowly he started to undo the gold laces. I put my other sandaled foot on his other knee and slowly eased his knees apart, and then I placed one foot on his crotch. Danny inhaled sharply, but he didn't stop what he was doing. He eased my foot out of the shoe, which he dropped into the box. As I rubbed my foot into his hardening crotch he lifted my bare foot and slipped my toes into his mouth. No one had ever done that to me, and it was my turn to catch my breath. When he started licking in between each toe, I couldn't stop myself from moaning. If this was how good it felt to get your toes sucked, Danny and I would be seeing more of each other.

After he'd sucked each one of my toes he lifted my foot up and slipped the heel into his mouth, nibbling at it lightly. He then tongued the bottom of my foot. I'd never felt anything like this before. By now Danny had a nice big hard-on in his pants. Every time I ground my shoe into his crotch he'd moan into my foot.

He finally eased my foot down onto his crotch and lifted my other foot from his crotch onto his knee. My

bare foot was slick from his tongue, and I ground it into his crotch wiggling my toes. Danny could barely undo the laces of my other shoe. His eyes were closed, and he was moaning loudly. By the time he'd unlaced that sandal and slipped the toes of that foot into his mouth, I knew he was close to coming.

I'd never gotten anyone off with just my feet before. I have to admit, I was getting pretty hot from the feel of my toes in Danny's mouth. He was sucking on them like they were my clit. I was so hot that I slipped a finger between my legs and fingered myself. I couldn't believe how wet I was.

The sight of me with my fingers between my legs and my toes in his mouth pushed Danny over the edge; he moaned and shuddered, and I could feel his dick jerking in his pants and the wet cum against my toes. Watching him come made me come as I slipped two fingers deep inside myself and came harder than I've ever come before.

Who knew shoe shopping could be so much fun?

I've worked my ass off to become a successful physician. I love my job and I love the benefits that come with being a good-looking, single male doctor.

I'm forty-two, never married, and I've always had beautiful girlfriends. Anna, my last girlfriend, was only nineteen and my office assistant. She was model beautiful, tall, thin, and half Spanish. I love exotic girls, and Anna was more gorgeous than most Spanish movie stars. Her waist-length dark hair, amazing hazel eyes, and great legs got me hot every time I looked at her. It didn't hurt that she loved wearing short skirts and tight tops that showed off her big tits either. Anna moved away for college last month. But before she left she gave me the best going-away present.

It was the night before her plane left for out of state. Anna was crying, telling me how sorry she was for leaving me. I dried her tears and told her that I'd miss her but that the feel of her mouth on my cock would help me to remember her. Even though she was only nineteen she really knew how to handle cock. With a big smile, Anna sat me in a chair, got down on her knees, and started to unbuckle my belt. I was hard before my pants were even off. I guess it hadn't occurred to me how much I really would miss Anna. She was beautiful, bright, an excellent assistant, and great in bed.

When Anna had gotten my pants down, she took my cock in her hands and slipped it into her mouth. Sucking me deep into the back of her throat, she started to pleasure me. Her tight little mouth and her tongue running across the tip of my dick were so hot. When I looked down, I could see her gorgeous tits bobbing up and down in her low-cut blouse. I grabbed her long hair and moved her head back and forth on my cock, just the way I wanted it. Whenever I pulled her mouth away from my dick, I could see her spit all over my cock. It was so sexy. Anna used her hand to tease the bottom of my dick and balls as she deep-throated me. I

leaned back and enjoyed watching Anna sucking me off until I came hard in her mouth. I almost came again watching her swallow every drop. "Mmm," she said as she licked her lips. She'd really given me something to remember.

Boy, will I miss my sweet Spanish girl. . . .

Every February my girlfriends and I take a road trip from the Bay Area to Las Vegas. February is the best time of the year because that's when Vegas has all the big conventions and the city is packed. Jessie and I are sales reps, and our friend Kristin is an exotic dancer. Our little crew always gets a lot of attention. But no matter what trouble we find ourselves in, we always take care of one another.

They say Las Vegas is Sin City, and I'd have to agree, especially after my last week with the girls at the Mirage. Vegas makes me do things I wouldn't normally do. Our second night there, Jessie and I got totally wasted and gambled away most of our cash on roulette—Damn you, red! We still had five days left to party and no gas money to get home!

Knowing that Kristin makes good money at her club back home, I begged for a loan. She told me that she'd also gotten a little carried away with her spending cash and had been hoping that I might lend *her* a few bucks.

Hmm, guess again, I told her, laughing. The three of us went to the bar and tried to figure out what we were going to do over Red Bull and vodkas. All of a sudden I had a great idea. I turned to Kristin. "You're going to have to take one for the team. You need to go shake it at one of these famous strip clubs and make us some money." Kristin's look said, This is supposed to be my vacation, too. But she knew it was the only way to make quick cash, so she agreed, but only if we promised not leave her alone in the club.

When we found our club of choice, Kristin went on-stage for her audition, which she nailed, of course. Jessie and I then got comfortable in a booth as Kristin got ready for her six-hour shift.

I'd never been to a strip club before; there were so many beautiful half-naked women everywhere. When Kristin got onstage all dolled up and wearing her come-fuck-me heels, my mouth hung open. She looked hot! As the night wore on Kristin made sure that Jessie and I

were comped drinks. Kristin had told us that girls come from all over the world to work in the club! But I still couldn't believe all the gorgeous girls working there. By five A.M., Kristin was finished with her shift and she'd made plenty of money. She asked if we could share a cab with Angie, a beautiful blonde girl from Brazil who was also staying at the Mirage. "No problem," I said, "the more the merrier."

We were drunk and giggling on the cab ride back to the hotel and insisted that Angie come up to our room for a drink. As soon as we got there we all stripped down to our tanks and panties and got cozy in our big queen-size beds. Angie was going to sleep over since she was staying in the other tower. It was Jessie and me in one bed, Kristin and Angie in the other. As soon as the lights went off, Jessie started laughing and tickling me. Then she reached her hand between my thighs and softly rubbed my pussy. I was a little weirded out, but I'd had too many drinks to think clearly. Plus, I kinda liked it. I'd always thought Jessie was gorgeous, and I knew it was all in good clean fun. Either way, what happens in Vegas, stays in Vegas.

I turned to face her and pressed my almost naked

body against hers and slid my tongue into her mouth. We then started full on making out. By now Jessie had slipped her hand into my panties and was softly rubbing my clit. I moaned and pushed her tank up and started rubbing her titties. Hers are so much bigger than mine, and I'd always admired them. Her nipples were so hard, I sucked on one first, then the other, swirling my tongue around them, until she started to press her hips against me.

Jessie took her hand out of my panties and, grabbing the back of my head, forced me down between her thighs as she lay back and spread her legs. She tasted sweet. I sucked on her clit. I was new to this bi stuff, but Jessie seemed like she was a pro as she turned me over, spread my legs wide, and slipped her fingers inside me. She had my shirt up and was licking and sucking on my tits. I was so turned on I wanted to scream, but I didn't want to wake the other girls.

By now Jessie was finger-fucking me with one hand and rubbing and squeezing my tits with the other. It felt so good I was close to coming. I quickly covered my mouth with my hand. When Jessie slipped her fingers

out and started rubbing my clit, I lost it. I came so hard against her fingers that my whole body shook with pleasure, and I could feel the cum run down my thighs.

Mmm. It was a whole new orgasm for me. I guess you learn something new every day.

I've been practicing ballet and dance since I was very young. It helps me stay in great shape and makes me very flexible. But my knees and back ache from many hours of hard practice and dancing. So for the past few months I've been going to a chiropractor for adjustments. I find a little tweaking here and there makes me feel a lot better.

Dr. James is my super-hot chiropractor. He's thirty-three and looks just like Brad Pitt. We always flirt with each other, but he's usually pretty professional. I say "usually" because last Wednesday our flirting went to a whole new level.

I'm five feet five inches tall and love wearing sexy threads whenever I can. Unfortunately, I rarely get the chance to show off my tight, sexy body because I'm usually in dance

sweats. But whenever I get the opportunity to throw on a miniskirt, tight white wife beater, and heels . . . I'm there. And that's exactly what I was wearing last Wednesday!

My session with Dr. James started out normally, me lying on one side and him with one hand on my lower back and the other hand on my shoulder. He adjusts one side, then I flip, and he adjusts my other side. But this time when I turned toward him, I caught him staring at my tits. I'm sure he'd been looking at my tight ass when he was working on my other side. I wasn't upset; actually, I kinda liked the attention. So, like the naughty twenty-two-year-old I am, I flaunted my assets. Since I was lying on my side, I could squeeze my upper arms together to make my C cups look even bigger. My nipples were rock hard, and I knew Dr. James could see them.

"Dr. James, are you okay? You're sweating," I said innocently. "Umm . . . Kat, it's just . . . you look so beautiful today," he said, flustered. "What can I say, Kat? You caught me."

That's all he had to say to turn me on. Just knowing that Dr. James was thinking dirty thoughts about

me was making my pussy wet. It turned me on even more that I'd caught him. With a shocked look on my face I said, "Dr. James, please. Get back to work." But I made sure to push my tits up against his arm as he adjusted me.

He started rubbing my shoulders and neck in a very nonprofessional way, and it was starting to feel too good. I lay there trying to keep from moaning. As Dr. James "casually" rubbed my neck and shoulders, he slowly and "casually" started rubbing my breasts. He was pretending it was routine, and I played right along. He had expert hands. When he started rubbing my nipples, pinching one then the other, my pussy started twitching, and I worried that I was soaking the table. I told him my thighs were aching and asked if he could rub them. I was hoping that he would "accidentally" feel the wetness between my legs as he did so.

Dr. James *very* slowly slid his hand up my short skirt. "Is this where you're sore, Kat?" he asked, rubbing my inner thighs. "Actually, it's a little higher," I answered. I slid onto my back, and without hesitation he slid his hand to my crotch, working his fingers into my panties. When he touched my clit, I groaned softly. "Do you like

that, Kat?" he asked, and I smiled. He then positioned himself between my legs, pushed my skirt up over my hips, and pulled my panties down. I didn't say a word. When he started licking my cunt, I ground my hips into his face and moaned with pleasure. I knew he wouldn't be able to take much more of this torture, and I was right. Dr. James unbuckled his belt, kicked off his shoes, and stepped out of his pants and underwear. He then got up on the table with me and rubbed the head of his cock on my clit. He was breathing quickly, and I could tell he wanted to fuck me hard right then. I "casually" rubbed his cock a little lower so he could feel my wet pussy on his dick. "Oh, God, Kat . . . please," he begged. "Please let me fuck you."

When I guided his cock into my tight pussy, Dr. James shoved it in and started fucking me hard and fast. I was getting a burn from the plastic table, but I loved it. "Fuck me harder!" I yelled. Dr. James rammed his hips against me as he fucked me even harder. It felt so good, I was close to coming. I could tell Dr. James was, too.

When I slid my hand down to his cock and squeezed, he groaned, "Oh, God, Kat, I'm gonna come, come with me."

My pussy muscles contracted, and I started trembling and coming all at once. Dr. James then pulled his cock out and squirted his cum all over my wet cunt.

Now, that's a great adjustment.

Once upon time, there was a gorgeous man named Kurt, who was very popular with the ladies. They loved his perfectly structured face, sky blue eyes, and that oh-so-sexy dimple in his left cheek, which drove them crazy when he smiled. But Kurt was too shy to realize it.

Kurt was a superintendent for a local construction company. Every few days he'd go to a big corporate building downtown to do maintenance work. He especially loved going to the twenty-seventh floor, where he got to see the beautiful, busty brunette, Heather. Heather was the front-desk girl for a large corporation. She was always professional and a little bit uptight. She had the poor construction workers constantly running around fixing

even the smallest problem. But there was something about her that just drove Kurt crazy.

"Morning, Heather," Kurt said one day with a huge smile.

Heather barely looked up at him. "Hey, while you're here, can you fix the sliding door to the storage room? It keeps getting stuck," she said.

"You betcha," he said. "Nice to see you, too." He smiled again, his dimple visible in his cheek.

Heather got up from her desk and walked Kurt to the storage room to show him the problem. When he checked, there was nothing wrong with the door. It worked just fine. "Well, I don't know why it works now. It was getting stuck all day yesterday," Heather explained. "Look, I'll show you." She then stepped inside the small storage room and slid the door back and forth. "Here, let me try," Kurt said, stepping into the storage room.

He fiddled with the door and pushed it closed. When he tried to open it, it was stuck! As Kurt tried his best to get them out, Heather sat on the stepladder and laughed.

"Why are you laughing? Do you think this is funny?" he asked.

"No, I find you funny. I don't really want you to fix the door. Well, not yet, anyway," she said.

"Oh, yeah? Why's that?" Kurt said, confused.

"That door's been broken from the first day I started working here. I thought we could talk in here for a minute." Then she grabbed Kurt's belt and pulled him close.

Kurt suddenly felt intimidated. He pulled away and said, "Let me work on getting us out of here. You need to get back to your desk."

Heather smiled and said, "It's lunchtime, plus no one ever comes back here." She then unbuttoned her black silk blouse. She was wearing a sexy black lace bra, and she had the most beautiful breasts Kurt had ever seen. When she unclasped the front of her bra and her tits spilled out, Kurt almost came right there. Heather took Kurt's big rough hands and put them on her breasts. Her nipples were getting hard in his hands. When Heather saw the crotch of his pants bulging, she knew she had him right where she wanted him.

"Do you like my breasts, Kurt? You can play with them," she said.

Kurt's heart started racing, and although he couldn't

believe it was really happening, he started kneading Heather's breasts, rubbing them together and pulling on her nipples. Heather was leaning against the wall of the storage room, moaning. Kurt started kissing Heather, forcing his tongue into her mouth and sucking hard on her lips. Heather pulled away and found the buckle of his pants. She slid her tight skirt up over her knees and knelt down to take his cock in her mouth.

Kurt couldn't believe Heather was sucking his dick. It was a dream come true. In the darkness he could just make her out. She was deep-throating him, licking and sucking while she played with his balls with her other hand.

"Oh, yeah . . . That feels good. Keep going," he groaned.

She sucked harder, tonguing the tip of his dick and then sucking him deep into the back of her throat. When she started licking his balls, he couldn't take it anymore. He lifted Heather up, pulled her skirt over her hips, yanked down her lacy panties, and sat her on the stepladder. He then grabbed his throbbing dick and roughly shoved it inside Heather's wet pussy, making her moan.

"I've wanted to fuck you for so long," she groaned.

That turned Kurt on even more. He couldn't believe what he was hearing . . . or doing!

"Fuck me harder, construction boy," she whispered.

Kurt grabbed Heather's firm ass and shoved his dick deep inside. He started fucking Heather hard and fast, pulling his dick almost out and then ramming it back in, banging her head against the wall as the stepladder rocked back and forth. Heather locked her legs around his hips and moaned with pleasure.

"Oh, Heather, I'm going to come. I want cum all over your chest."

When she pulled the sides of her shirt farther apart, Kurt pulled out and shot his cum between her breasts.

Heather's body was shaking. "I'm coming, too," she moaned, and she came so hard she almost fell off the stepladder.

When they'd caught their breath, they cleaned up their naughty mess and fixed their clothes, agreeing not to tell a soul.

"Now you can fix the door." Heather said, smiling.

Antonio is my hot Italian friend I often go on trips with. He's got a gorgeous tan that seems to glow all day and a set of perfect teeth you notice at the first smile. For someone as wealthy and good-looking as Antonio, you'd think he could have just about any woman he wanted, and he often does. I think he just likes playing the field and isn't ready to settle down.

Last week, after seeing me with Antonio, my close friend Jackie told me she thought he was ridiculously hot and asked if I could introduce them. Knowing what a womanizer Antonio is, I knew he would be all over Jackie in a heartbeat. I tried to warn Jackie of Antonio's bad behavior, but the less highly I spoke of him, the more turned on she became. To be honest, I think Jackie just wanted to fuck him.

I arranged for the three of us to have lunch on Antonio's yacht the following week. When we got together, it was a picture-perfect Miami day. I wore a little white sundress that blew gracefully in the light wind, and Jackie wore tight pants and a gold bikini top that showed off her new C cups. No doubt about it, Jackie looked hot. But God, Antonio, shirtless and wearing white linen pants, looked just as yummy as Jackie.

After a delicious lunch on deck, Antonio gave us the "grand tour" of the yacht. When we got to the master bedroom, it was beautiful with large windows for ocean views. With a big smile Jackie sat down on the king-size bed and beckoned me over. "Becki, come sit next to me," she said. I knew I was a glass of white wine away from a threesome.

I sat on the bed next to Jackie as she slipped out of her bathing suit top and asked me what I thought of her new breasts. I said they were perfect, and I asked if I could touch them. Jackie took my hand and put it on her breast as she leaned toward me for a kiss.

I softly touched her as she kissed me. It was different kissing a woman. Jackie's lips were so soft and her

tongue gentle. I unzipped her pants and slipped her out of them. She wasn't wearing panties, and her pussy was completely shaved. I was so turned on. I got down on my knees on the floor between Jackie's legs and pulled her hips toward me so I could lick from her stomach to her clit. "Mmm. Antonio, would you like to join us?" Jackie moaned, massaging her breasts.

Antonio, who'd been watching us from the doorway, smiled and came over to the bed. He stood over us for a few moments rubbing his cock. When he was good and hard, he pulled his pants down to his ankles. He then took his fat penis and slid it into Jackie's waiting mouth. While she sucked him off, he rubbed my hair as I sucked my friend's hot cunt.

Antonio's moans were driving me crazy. When I couldn't take it anymore, I stood up, took off my dress, and got on top of Jackie. She took her mouth off Antonio's dick, lay back on the bed, and started licking my breasts and nipples.

Antonio walked behind me as I straddled Jackie. He lifted my hips up and started fingering my clit. When his finger was good and wet, he slid it into my ass, fin-

ger-fucking me with long strokes as Jackie licked and sucked my tits. It felt too good. "Please fuck me!" I begged, wanting the real thing.

He positioned himself behind me and shoved himself in me hard. My small tits where all over Jackie's face as she squeezed and sucked on my nipples. It felt so good as Antonio held my hips tight, fucking me hard, pulling out and then ramming his dick back deep inside me. The feel of Jackie's mouth was driving me over the edge. After a few moments I came all over Antonio's dick.

I was exhausted and felt so good, but I knew I still had to take care of my friends, so I got on the bed behind Jackie and started sucking her big juicy tits as Antonio slid himself inside her wet pussy. She moaned and writhed on the bed, pushing her hips up toward him. As Antonio fucked her good and hard, I massaged and squeezed her tits together, pinching the nipples and sucking on them. I could tell they were both getting close to coming. Jackie moaned loudly, then bucked her hips under Antonio, who was groaning as he pulled out and came all over her sexy stomach.

We all lay on the bed breathing heavily. The windows were fogged up, and I don't think any of us believed what had just happened. Of course everything happens for a reason, and we were all pleased. Before we left the boat we scheduled lunch for next week, too!

There's no better job than owning your own tattoo parlor out here on the ocean in sunny San Diego, where seeing half-naked girls is as common as the sunset. Being the horny thirty-nine-year-old man I am, I love it.

Every day beautiful women come into the shop wearing tiny string bikinis and flaunting their assets. Most of them want what I call the tramp stamp—you know, a tattoo on the lower back, usually a tribal or zodiac sign. I hate ruining their gorgeous backs with tattoos they might regret in five years. But my job is to make sure the client is happy when they walk out my door. That's exactly what I did to Suzie Q.

Suzie Q is a natural beauty. She has that perfect next-door, beach-girl look. She's tall, with long white-blond hair down

to her ass, ocean-blue eyes, and a great year-round summer tan. The guys all know her because she's dated quite a few professional boarders who get their artwork done at the parlor.

When the striking blonde came in last weekend for her tramp stamp, she was wearing a teal bikini top and tiny white miniskirt that showed off her long legs. I treated her just like anyone else, and I think she was annoyed by it. I could tell Suzie was used to getting her way. She even gave me some attitude, like, Don't you know who I am. When that didn't work, she started flirting with me, trying to get a response. But again, I treated her like everybody else, even though I was trying to hide the tent I was pitching inside my pants.

"Arch your back a little more so we get this tat right," I casually told her, starting my work. Suzie arched her back, sticking her tight little ass up in the air. I could see the bottoms of her ass cheeks hanging out of her tiny skirt. It was so hot.

"How's this, Doug?" she asked with a slight giggle.

I knew this girl was trying to flirt with me just because I wouldn't give her the time of day. My sick plan

was working. (It actually has an 85 percent success rate when done right.)

I had just put the final touches on Suzie and had removed my rubber gloves when she took my hand and placed it under her skirt on her ass. I looked over the top of my station to make sure no one was nearby to hear us. Oh, my God, did I want this girl! Sooo sexy! And her ass felt as good as it looked, too.

She kept making small moans and pushing her ass into my hand. My dick was getting as hard as a rock, so I decided to teach Suzie a lesson. I pushed her skirt over her hips, pulled down her panties, and started rubbing her hot little clit. When she was good and wet, I stuck two fingers into her puss and started finger-fucking her with deep thrusts, pulling my fingers almost all the way and then ramming them back in.

She moaned so loudly that I held her face down on the towel to muffle the noise. Her groans were turning me on. Her tight pussy was getting wetter and wetter, dripping down my fingers to the table. The harder I fucked her, the more she moaned and bucked her hips. I couldn't take it anymore. I slid my fingers out of her

and stood in front of the table. I then undid my pants, lifted Suzie's face from the towel, and shoved my cock in her mouth until she was gagging. I figured that would teach her to be so spoiled.

"That's right, suck it, you slut." I moaned as Suzie deep-throated me. "Don't stop." I said, holding her head and shoving my cock in and out of her mouth. Her spit was all over me, and it turned me on so much that I couldn't hold back any longer. I pulled out and came all over her sexy ass.

But I wasn't finished with Suzie yet. She'd been a good girl and I was gonna make her come. I pulled her to the back of the table and lifted her hips up until she was on her knees. I spread her wet pussy lips and sucked hard on her pretty little clit. I covered her mouth with my hand to keep her in quiet. I sucked harder and harder as she moaned into my hand, then, when she was close to coming, I stuck my finger deep inside her and wiggled it around. When she started trembling and breathing heavily, I knew she was going to come all over my face . . . if I was lucky.

"Come on, baby. Come on my face, you slut. Come on!"

I could tell she'd never had it like this before; Suzie had the most intense orgasm I've ever seen as she collapsed trembling on the table. My fingers were soaked, and I swear she tasted like honey.

The funny thing is that when she was leaving, she gave me a look like she'd won. As though she'd known all along I wanted to come onto her. She was half right; it was more like I wanted come on her.

I have another appointment with Suzie next week, and she can feel free to use me like a dirty towel, if she wants to.

Should you fix your hair and makeup before you go to the gym? Definitely, if Jack, the hottest trainer alive, works there! I can tell he takes really good care of himself. He's at least six feet two inches, with a sexy muscled body, perfect beach blond hair, and, to top it off, emerald green eyes. I'm nothing special, but since I stay in shape and have big blue eyes and long blond hair, I always get attention. I guess being twenty-two doesn't hurt either.

I work at a spa part-time, but I'm a student and don't make a lot of money. I really wanted to sign up for some private training sessions with Jack. The going rate at my gym is about $250 for six sessions. That's way out of my budget, but I knew that if I could get the money from my dad, Jack would love meeting and training me.

I'll admit it: I'm spoiled, and Daddy was happy to give me the money. He was glad that I was working part-time and taking care of myself. I was so excited when I signed up with Jack the next morning. When he walked over to greet me, I almost died. Oh, my God, he was even more perfect up close! I told Jack that my thighs were my biggest concern and that whenever I worked them they got really sore so I would give up. He said he doesn't train quitters, then he gave me a tip. He said that if I were to rub my inner thighs nightly before bed, it would help relieve the soreness.

At our next training session Jack asked how my thighs were doing. I explained to him that I must have been rubbing them the wrong way because they were very sore today. Jack sat me on a bench and started rubbing my thighs. "How does this feel?" he asked. "You have to rub really deeply to loosen up the sore muscles." Mmm. It felt so good to have him touching my legs. I could feel there was a little bit of flirting going on between us. Jack started rubbing farther up my thighs. He then turned me over and started kneading the muscles in my ass. He said that the muscles in my legs were connected to those in my butt and that sometimes it

helped to rub there as well. When he asked if I would be up for soaking with him in the gym's hot tub later, after he was done with his clients, I didn't hesitate. Of course I was all over it! Alone time with Jack that I wasn't paying for—how cool was that?

We met up a few hours later in the private trainer's room. I was wearing my tiniest bikini, and Jack was in a sexy pair of dark blue trunks. After a few minutes of flirting and splashing in the hot tub, Jack led me to a bench and laid me facedown on a towel; he then started to massage my inner thighs. He said he didn't want me to be sore tonight and would show me the right way to rub them. It felt so good that I was actually getting horny just from his massage. "Mmm," I moaned, hoping he'd get the hint as I slid his hand up my thigh toward my tight pussy. He got the hint and slowly pulled off my bikini bottoms. He then spread my legs, opened my pussy lips, and slid two wet fingers inside me. I moaned and lifted my hips to give him easier access.

Jack spread my legs wider and started to finger-fuck me with one hand while he rubbed my clit with the other. It felt so good, I knew I was gonna come any second. Jack fucked my pussy hard, and when he wasn't

stroking my clit, he was spreading my ass cheeks. When he stuck his face between my cheeks and licked my clit, I came so hard I almost fell off the bench. Jack laughed and turned me around to face him. I knew what he wanted. I licked the palm of my hand, took his hard cock out of his trunks, and started rubbing it with my right hand. I then added my left hand to make sure he was getting a good hand job. I could see by the look in his eyes that he was. I then got down on my knees and took his dick deep in my mouth and started sucking his cock hard and fast.

After I couldn't take it anymore I stood up, sat facing him on his lap, and shoved his cock inside me. Jack grabbed my hips and started bouncing me up and down really hard. It was a wonderful pain. I was close to coming again, and I could feel that Jack was, too. His dirty words pushed me over the edge. "I love your tight pussy," he moaned, as he shot deep inside me.

Right after college I got a part-time job at my local grocery store. I figured I'd better start saving now for my big move to Hollywood at the end of summer.

I'm an actor and hope to make it big someday.

I'm good-looking and pretty muscular. I stand about six feet three inches, so the store manager mostly puts me in the back room to do the stocking. It's not really exciting, but hey, it's a job. After a month working with the same crew, we had a newbie, a hot one. Rachel was a long-legged foreign-exchange student from France with the face of an angel. She had smooth, fair skin, sexy blond hair, and eyes the color of root beer. I'm a sucker for big brown eyes, and I couldn't wait to introduce myself to her.

The following week, after everyone had cooled down about "hot Rachel," I begged my boss to let me out of the back room for one night to work in produce with Rachel. I just had to talk to her! I was lucky and caught a break. Someone had called in sick from produce, so I'd get to work with Rachel, and she and I would close the store. I was so stoked! I could barely contain myself as I put on my apron and headed toward the produce section with a big smile on my face.

"Well, hello there. You must be Rachel?" I said, trying not to be corny.

"Yeah, that's me. Hope you know your fruit," she said in her sexy French accent.

Oh God, just hearing her voice made me want to bend her over the apples right then and there and fuck her hard. I tried to stay cool.

"Well, actually, I'm Brian, the stock boy. I've never worked in produce before. Maybe you can show me a thing or two," I said.

I could tell she thought I was cute. That's when the flirting started. When we were spraying down the vegetables, she hosed me pretty good. The flirting got more intense, and all I could think about was how hot

Rachel would sound getting fucked. That accent of hers was really doing it for me. I was so blown away by how pretty and sexy she was that I could barely pay attention to what I was doing. At closing time I locked the doors so Rachel and I could finish our duties.

"I could use some assistance from a stock boy back here," she yelled from the stockroom.

I headed into the back room, where Rachel was taking off her apron. I walked up to her and asked what she needed help with.

"Well, first you can help me move these big boxes out of the way. Then you can help me undo the knot of this stubborn apron."

I moved the boxes and then stood behind her to undo the knot. When I unraveled the knot, she turned around and pushed me up against the wall. I could barely catch my breath. I was pleasantly shocked by how Rachel was coming on to me. She placed my hands on her hips and started to suck on my neck. I couldn't believe it. All I had been thinking about all day was fucking this hot European, and here she was kissing me. At this point my dick was so hard I had to get it out of my pants. Rachel unzipped her tight jeans and wig-

gled out of them. She then pulled her white baby tee over her head. Her tits were full and firm. She then said, "I have a surprise for you," as she lay back on the worktable.

I anxiously came toward her as she took a large green cucumber from a produce box. She then softly rubbed it across her clit, using her left hand to rub her beautiful tits. This couldn't be happening. I'd seen stuff like this only in the movies. She was such a tease. I watched Rachel for a few minutes, then I straddled her and began to lick and suck on her juicy tits. I then took the cucumber and started sliding it in and out of her tight twat. She was such a dirty little slut that I had to give it to her. I started fucking her harder and harder with the cucumber as I squeezed her tits.

"Oh, yes, Brian!" she yelled.

I couldn't take it anymore. I pushed the cucumber into her mouth and told her to be quiet, turned Rachel over on all fours, pulled out my cock, and started to fuck her hard. When she looked back at me with those big brown eyes and started moaning, I lost all concentration and blew my load all over the back of her ass.

"You are such a dirty, dirty girl, Rachel," I said, out of breath.

Rachel sat up on the table fixing her clothes and said with a smile, "Tomorrow you will bring the strawberries, and I will come first."

It turned out to be my best summer job ever.

I go to a private school in upstate Maine. It's a very large school and has cheerleading, football, base-ball, and even soccer. Cheerleading was the only thing that interested me, though. Cheering and my boyfriend, Peter, that is.

Last Saturday night Peter totally ditched me after the football game to go hang out with his friends. I was so bummed. We'd had plans for after the game, and I'd worked really hard on looking great for him. I had my long brown hair in sexy curls, and I'd high-lighted my green eyes with sparkles on my eyelids. I even wore my best push-up bra under my uniform.

I was so upset that I sat on the field bench and cried for about fifteen minutes until my friend Roger came over with a tissue. He assists the players and the coach. Roger's a great

guy. He and I have been friends since our freshman year, but we don't see much of each other because we hang with different crowds at our school. He's the type of person to whom I can tell anything, and he'll understand.

Roger, who'd seen what had happened with my boyfriend, handed me the tissue and told me that I was too good for Peter. I was so sad to hear that. That's exactly what my parents have been telling me for months. I felt naive and stupid for wanting to be with someone so selfish. Then I got angry and I wanted to get even with Peter for hurting me once again.

Roger moved my pom-poms to the other side of the bench and scooted closer. He put his left hand on my upper thigh and stroked it softly as we talked. It felt pretty good, so I didn't ask him to stop. And I'll admit, having someone there to comfort me made me feel a lot better.

As he rubbed my leg, he slowly and very casually reached up my skirt and started rubbing my pussy over my panties. Oh my goodness! Just knowing I shouldn't be doing it turned me on even more. I knew I should tell him to stop, but he was being so sweet and was making me feel better. And I have to admit, I was still mad at Peter.

I slowly spread my legs so he could reach his fingers inside my panties. Roger slid his hand farther up my thigh, slipped a finger inside my panties, and started fingering me.

I knew I should say something, but it felt so good, and Roger and I were friends. When I didn't say anything, he got on his knees between my legs, pulled off my panties, and opened my legs spread eagle. He then started licking my pussy as I sat with my legs widely spread on the bench.

"Mmm, you taste like candy," he said, looking up at me with a big smile on his face.

I was so turned on. When I pulled my knees up to my chin, Roger slipped another finger inside me. I was dripping wet. I wanted to come so badly. I started shaking from the pleasure he was giving me. It was so hot to be getting eaten in public and from Roger. I moaned louder as he slid his finger in and out of my pussy and roughly licked my clit. I grabbed the back of his head and forced his mouth tighter on my clit. Oh, it felt so good. I could feel I was close to coming.

"Yeah, here it comes.... I'm going to come.... I'm coming.... I'm coming." I moaned as my

whole body shook, and I came shaking all over Roger's face.

I had cum everywhere. I was such a mess, but it wasn't going to stop me from sucking Roger off and letting him come all over me. I owed him that for making me feel so much better.

I sat Roger on the bench, unzipped his pants, and pulled out his cock. I massaged him in my palms for a few minutes, working his balls with my hands. Then I started giving his dick long wet licks before sucking him into my mouth. Roger moaned and grabbed the back of my head, holding it against his dick. I slid my mouth off his dick and then licked him and then sucked hard, pulling him deep into the back of my throat. Then I slid him out of my mouth and licked all around the head, giving him little kisses before sucking him deeply into my throat again. When I heard Roger groaning and felt him buck his hips off the bench, I knew he was close to coming. I didn't want to miss a drop. I gave the tip one last kiss, then I sucked him into my mouth while massaging his balls. When Roger started coming, I didn't miss a bit. Mmm, I felt so much better. And I hadn't thought once about Peter.

I live by the bay in San Francisco, and it seems like everyone here is as into art as I am. I've been oil painting and sketching since I was a kid, and now I'm getting into clay sculpting.

I know when you see a six-foot-four-inch college football player you don't really think he's an artist. But it's who I am. I recently dropped into a live nude modeling class. I'd never been to one before, but I had heard great things about it. I was hoping that it would help me to concentrate even more on capturing the human form on paper, and I knew no one would judge me there.

When I walked into the low-key studio, I was surprised to see how gorgeous the live model was. When she walked out from the back, stood up on a white square box, and dropped

her robe, my mouth fell open. She was hot. She was Asian, with the smoothest skin I'd ever seen. Her long jet-black hair was loose and fell down to her ass, and her deep dark eyes were highlighted with smudged black eyeliner. Her breasts weren't big, but they were full and perky with dark nipples. The hair at the triangle between her legs was also inky black. It was her mouth that turned me on the most; her lips were full and sexy and deep red. God, she was the sexiest woman I had ever laid eyes on. Her name was Lu. She then sat on the platform and posed with both knees up just barely covering her breasts.

The class was small, with only eleven students, and I knew she would see me. A guy as tall as I am, and, if I do say so myself, as good-looking, really stands out.

I set down with my art pallet ready to go, but I couldn't concentrate because of Lu's beauty. I just couldn't stop staring, and I can't stare *and* draw at the same time. It didn't help that when she picked something to concentrate on for the class, it turned out to be me.

I swear she was staring right at me. When she licked her sexy red lips, I almost dropped my pencil. When she

adjusted her knee a little, I could see the outline of her full right breast. With her knees drawn up to her chest I could see her clit. It was so pink against the dark hair on her pussy. When she turned her head, her long black hair fell in a curtain across her shoulder. I was completely turned on by this exotic beauty. And her thick black eyeliner threw in just the right amount of sultriness. When I felt myself getting hard, I prayed that no one could see my erection. I was already embarrassed for myself. The bulge in my jeans was growing by the minute.

I tried to concentrate on something other than the gorgeous naked woman sitting in front of me. But thoughts of my aunt Betty were pushed away by Lu's sexy hips and thighs. I figured I would have to make the best of the day and gave her a big grin, hoping she'd come over to see her portrait at the end. I smiled at her and made a couple of goofy faces. It worked; she smiled a few times and even giggled softly once. After class she slipped on her robe and came over. She was even more beautiful up close. Her body, outlined by the sheer fabric of the robe, was even sexier than when she had been naked. When I showed her the portrait I'd managed to

draw, she gave me a big smile. With her perfect white teeth her smile was beautiful. My dick was throbbing and my mind was thinking all kinds of dirty thoughts involving Lu. I held my pallet to my body tightly. She smiled, took my hand, and asked me to take down her phone number.

"I think I insist on private sessions of nude sketching with you next time. You need more practice. . . . That's not what I look like at all," she said with a wink.

For my high school graduation, my parents decided to take me on a cruise to the Caribbean. I've wanted to go there since I was fourteen. What's not to love about the tropics? Everything is gorgeous: the weather, the ocean, the beaches—you name it. I was excited for months before the cruise. I was thrilled that my parents were so proud of me that they'd give me such a thoughtful and expensive graduation gift.

"We just want the best for you, Brooke," Daddy said, beaming when I thanked them.

When my vacation date had finally arrived, I made sure to pack my collection of hot bikinis and dancing shoes. I was going to make sure to put these legs to good use on the dance floor.

When I first saw the ship in the dock, I couldn't believe it. It must have been at least eleven stories high. It was beautiful. Then my parents gave me a second surprise: I would have my very own cabin. I couldn't believe they were actually treating me like an adult. And I had my own sundeck right outside. How fabulous was that?

That first night at dinner, I was amazed at how many good-looking men were onboard. Waiters, passengers, cooks—I couldn't believe my eyes! The last thing I wanted was to talk to some gorgeous man and later find out that I had broccoli stuck in my teeth. So I hardly touched my meal.

After I kissed Mom and Dad good night I headed back to my cabin to get dressed to impress. I decided on my little black kilt skirt, low-cut baby pink top, and my friend Jody's stripper heels. Pink always looks hot on blondes.

Being eighteen, I couldn't order alcohol, but I knew if I stood at the bar long enough in my short skirt and high heels, someone would order a drink for me. Sure enough, it wasn't long before I had *two* guys at my side.

Ryan was tall, dark, and sophisticated. Josh, who

looked like a surfer, was blond and muscular. Both were hot, just in different ways. They were college room-mates on vacation, and we talked for a while. After a few drinks, Josh invited me back to their room to party.

How could I deny those muscular arms and sexy tat-toos? I was pretty overwhelmed—I mean, not one, but *two* hot guys, and on my first night of the cruise. I didn't even have to think about it. "Sure, let's go," I said, tak-ing the last sip of my cranberry and vodka.

Their cabin was even nicer than mine.

"Relax . . . Make yourself comfortable." Josh said as he sat down next to me on the bed and gently rubbed my thigh. Ryan went to make cocktails at the bar.

I lay down on the bed and put my arms over my head, letting my skirt hike up and showing off my newly tanned thighs and my pink, lacy thong. I was just begging to get fucked. Some might call me crazy, but I knew exactly what I was doing.

Within seconds Ryan was sitting on the bed with Josh and me. My drinks had gone completely to my head, so I decided on putting on a little show for my new friends.

I slid off my thong, lay back, lifted my legs up on the

bed, and spread them far apart, resting one leg on Josh and the other on Ryan. I then slowly licked two fingers, slid them inside my pussy, and started fingering myself in front of the guys.

"Mmm," I moaned, writhing on the bed finger-fucking myself. When I looked up, I saw that both men had their pants open and were playing with their dicks. I got so hot watching them beat off to me. I began rubbing my clit with my fingers and playing with my nipples through my thin shirt. Oh God, I was so close to coming.

"I'm gonna come. I'm coming right now," I moaned, rubbing my clit harder and faster.

"Mmm . . . come, baby." Josh whispered, as both he and Ryan jerked off faster.

"Oh, oh," I moaned, coming so hard that I could feel the cream dripping down my ass cheeks.

I could tell both Josh and Ryan were close to coming as they beat off watching me; their dicks were rock hard and they were breathing very heavily. I turned around on the bed, got on all fours, and stuck my ass out, moving my skirt out of the way. They got up and stood on

either side of the bed jerking off, and then they came almost at the same time, right on my ass.

"Oh . . . that's so good," I moaned, feeling the hot cum on my cheeks.

What a great start to my vacation. I knew I'd be seeing a lot of these two guys.

I'm sure my dad would kill me, but hey . . . It's not like I had sex or anything.

My wife, Gabby, and I are newlyweds. Every day is so exciting for us as we learn new things about each other. We know we love the same type of music, TV shows, and food. In fact, we're so in sync that we even finish each other's sentences.

Before I met Gabby, I'd thought of myself as average, but she makes me feel so special. On the other hand, Gabby is anything but average! For one thing, she's gorgeous! Although she's petite, she has all the right curves in all the right places. But it's her face that gets everyone's attention. She has the most beautiful emerald green eyes and long dark eyelashes. And she has perfect light brown hair with soft curls at the ends. She looks even more beautiful early in the morning when she first wakes up.

I'm so in love with Gabby that I would do anything for her, including going to Tahoe in the winter, even though I think I'm allergic to snow and pine trees! She's been talking about taking a ski trip there for as long as I can remember.

Being the wonderful husband I am, I booked our trip to Tahoe. I really just wanted to spend time alone with her. Since the wedding it seems like we always have friends or family around. I couldn't wait to have her all to myself.

As soon as we arrived at our cabin Gabby wanted to go night skiing. I didn't even know there was such a thing, but hell, I'll try anything once.

Gabby put on the hottest fucking snow-bunny out-fit I have ever seen. She was decked out in light blue leggings, a white miniskirt, and white furry boots that matched perfectly. But I think it was her sexy low-cut sweater, exposing half her gorgeous tits, that did it for me. She looked so hot that I didn't even want to go ski-ing anymore.

Gabby managed to get us out of the cabin. But when we got to the slopes, I couldn't stop making the moves on my wife. She was driving me nuts! So I grabbed her

Making her scream for more. She was so moist, and the feeling was so intense.

"Come inside me, baby," Gabby whispered.

When she said that, I grabbed her by the hips, lifted her up, and forced myself deep inside her, pumping until I came.

When she came a moment later, I could feel her body shake while I was inside of her. It was the sexiest thing.

It was our best sex so far. I couldn't wait to do it all over again tonight in the cabin. High five on Tahoe!

My good friend Brad is a great clothing designer here in Santa Monica, trying to make it big. With his long dark hair, great body, and cut abs, if he wasn't a fashion designer he could be a model, he's so good-looking. Brad has been asking me to model for his new clothing line for some time now. I always say no because I don't think that I have what it takes. The last time he asked and I turned him down, he told me that I might not be six feet tall, but that I had an exotic "look" that he liked. He said most girls would kill to have turquoise-colored eyes and long jet-black hair. And at five feet nine inches, I'm taller than most men. Well, I must say, his charm worked; the next time he asked me to model for an upcoming project, I agreed. The photo shoot would be done at his home, where

he has a small studio. He asked me to come over Friday at five after work. As the week went by, I got more and more excited.

When Friday came, I made sure to arrive on time and with a big smile. Brad came to the door barefoot and very sexy, wearing worn-in jeans hanging low on his hips and a white T-shirt. He gave me a big smile and handed me my first wardrobe change. It was a black bikini top with matching booty shorts. The shorts had a big skull right across the ass! Typical Brad. When I was changed and my hair and makeup were finished, Brad put me in front of a white drop cloth and started shooting "casual" photos of me.

He started by taking close-up shots of my face. He kept talking to me, telling me I was beautiful and had a great body. He made me feel so pretty and at ease. I then sat on the arm of his sofa with my legs stretched out across the seat. I felt sexy, like a Victoria's Secret model.

"That's it," Brad said, stepping back and taking rapid shots. The sexier I acted, the more he liked it. I started caressing my shoulder, and then I let my hand slip down to my breasts, making my nipples hard. I then

moved my hand down my stomach and let it rest on my crotch.

"Mmm, that's it. Be sexy, baby. You're so sexy," Brad said.

I slid down onto the sofa and pulled my long hair out of the clip, letting it fall over the back of the sofa. I brought my knees up on the couch and slipped my other hand inside my shorts. I then started fingering my clit while looking straight into the camera. Brad could see everything; I knew it was killing him.

I was getting hotter and hotter. The more I thought of Brad watching me and taking photos, the hornier I got. I could feel myself getting wetter and wetter. I wanted to come so badly. When I heard Brad say, "Oh, yeah . . . That's it, baby, come for me," I knew it was okay. So I let go.

I closed my eyes and started rubbing my tits with one hand while I stroked my clit with the other. I was gonna make a mess in his clothes, but neither of us cared. When I slipped a finger inside my pussy, it was too much; I came with a big smile on my face. I knew Brad got some hot photos, so I didn't feel too bad for making him watch.

I started doing yoga last month. Now, I know yoga is good for you mentally and physically, and it helps tone your body, but I can't stand it! It bores me, all that breathing and chanting. I'm there only until I bang Nicole, the ridiculously hot instructor. After that, no more yoga. A guy in his mid-forties should be doing something else with his time, not chasing a twenty-one-year-old yoga instructor.

Nicole is new to Los Angeles. She's from Reno and is always saying how hard it is to make friends out here. It must be tough being so fuckin' hot, living in L.A.? Yeah, right.

Nicole stands about five feet seven inches tall, and weighs about a buck twenty-five. She's got sexy curly red hair, over-flowing 34D cups, and the most amazing body (I'm sure it's

from all the yoga). But it's those lips of hers, like ripe cherries waiting to be sucked on, that get me hot every time.

After class today I had hoped to ask Nicole out. She gives me the eye every now and then. And just the other day I swore she felt my dick when she was correcting my position. She's been driving me nuts with her big tits and her itty-bitty outfits.

But before I could even get a chance to ask Nicole out, she asked me to stay after class.

"I have something that might help you relax, Rick," Nicole told me when I walked in, before class started. I got nervous and shy, like she knew that I'd been think-ing about fucking her during classes.

When the session was over, she said good-bye to the rest of the class and locked the door. She then asked me to stretch with her to cool down. We had a nice friendly chat as we stretched, and then all of a sudden Nicole took off her top.

"Wait a minute. . . . What are you doing?" I asked. Not that I was complaining, but I had to pick up my jaw up from the floor.

"Naked yoga," she said casually. "Haven't you heard about it? All the celebrities here do it."

"Oh, yeah, of course I have," I lied, quickly yanking off my shirt.

When she took off the rest of her clothes, I took off mine. I was all over her little game. Next she put her left leg behind her head, then her right leg! Oh, my God! I was in heaven. She was completely shaved and had a pretty little pussy. Nicole should be appearing in *Playboy,* not teaching yoga.

She then licked her finger and casually started rubbing herself. Now, I know *this* isn't part of yoga!

She was slipping her finger in and out of her pussy and moaning softly. I couldn't take it anymore. I stood up and went over to her. With her feet still behind her head, I gently pushed her back on the floor and lifted her hips up. When she smiled, I knew I was on the right track. I reached for my hard dick and rubbed the head of it on her clit. It was so soft and smooth.

Nicole licked the palm of her hand, took my cock, and started stroking it. My dick was really hard now. I bent down and sucked her clit, sticking my tongue in

and out of her pussy until she started moaning. I wanted to feel her come, so I slipped two fingers into her sweet wet pussy and fingered her until she was groaning and trembling under me. When I sucked hard on her clit, she tensed up, then came shaking in my mouth.

Nicole sat up and gave me a big smile, then she slipped my throbbing cock into her mouth. Oh, it felt so good. She sucked hard on me, pulling my dick deep into her throat as she massaged my balls. I was so close, but I wanted to come all over her gorgeous tits. She gave me one long suck as she stroked me hard, then I pulled out of her mouth. I was in ecstasy as I shot my cum all over her. It was so sexy.

I felt like the luckiest man in the world. I couldn't believe what just happened. But what I really couldn't believe was that I'd decided I liked yoga and would continue taking classes.

It was the sixth-month anniversary for my boyfriend, Tommy, and me, and I wanted to make it special: something we'd remember all year.

Tommy loves the ocean. He was born to surf, and getting alone time with him away from the beach seemed almost impossible these days. That's why I planned a camping trip on the beach. I couldn't wait to surprise him. I knew I was truly in love because I was thinking about his wants and not mine.

On our anniversary, I told Tommy of my surprise I asked him to meet me at "our spot" at the beach. He was thrilled and told me he'd see me at eight P.M.

I rushed to our hidden beach spot to set up camp. As silly as it sounds, I thought Tommy might like seeing me

in a coconut shell bikini. I'm petite, only five feet two inches, but a sexy bikini always hugs me in the right spots. My soft brown hair falls to the middle of my back, and my golden highlights bring out my summer tan. My eyes are sea blue, and my caramel-colored skin makes any swimsuit look hot. I'd brought a cozy tent, marshmallows, hot dogs, and beer; tucked a flower in my hair; and started grilling the hot dogs over a small fire pit. What more could he ask for?

I'd worked really hard on everything and was pleased with the results. I really wanted Tommy to know how special he was to me.

He soon arrived. . . .

And just as I thought . . . my lover boy loved the surprise and was digging my new bikini. I was pleased with his reaction and looked forward to our evening alone. I had been planning it for weeks.

Tommy walked me closer to the ocean waves, and as soon as we sat down he started caressing my back with his soft fingers then untied my bikini top. My nipples grew hard from the cool ocean breeze. Chills went

down my spine as he massaged my breasts, gently laying me down on the sand. He kissed my neck and shoulders and then worked his way down my chest. I moaned softly. Tommy is very sexy to me. He's tall and muscular, with a tight surfer body. And he has a small happy trail that leads down to many good things. I was getting hotter and hotter, and my pussy ached. I so wanted to come. We rolled around in the sand kissing and hugging. Tommy rocked his hard body on top of me and ground his hips against mine, rubbing his hard cock against my clit. The sand added to the sexy friction, and I was soon soaking my bikini bottom. I couldn't believe how sexy just rubbing against each other could be.

Tommy was sucking hard on my nipples and rubbing his face between my breasts. He then slipped one leg between my thighs and ground his crotch into mine, rubbing his dick against me. I was so wet, and my clit was hard and had started to quiver. I wrapped my legs against Tommy's waist and pushed my hips against him. I could feel that he was close to coming; his breathing was heavy and he was squeezing my breasts

tightly. I was so turned on by us making out. I squeezed my legs around Tommy's waist. I was about to come, when I felt him tighten up and come against my legs. A moment later I came, too.

What a great anniversary.

This is DJ Scotty and you're listening to WKZZ."

Every night from five to ten P.M. I hear those words from my stereo. WKZZ is a rock station out here in L.A. I've become obsessed with DJ Scotty and his deep, sexy voice. For the last eight months at least, his voice has been making me horny. I think about him and what he might look like every day. I've never wanted so badly to meet someone because of his voice. Let alone a radio DJ.

I'm twenty-four years old, with cocoa eyes, pouty lips, shoulder-length blond hair that I keep curly, and a 34C cup size. I could pretty much get any man I wanted. But I've never heard a voice like his before.

Then one night, I heard the words: "The first two people

to come down to my studio on West Fourth Street decked out in their best eighties outfit will win two tickets to tonight's sold-out concert!"

That was it. I had tons of eighties gear. I just had to hurry so I could be one of the first two.

I put on a ripped wife beater that hung off one shoulder and paired it with a super-short miniskirt and classic eighties neon pink, high-heeled pumps. I crimped my blond hair, teased it out, and slipped on some chunky bracelets and hoop earrings. I was like totally eighties!

I rushed to WKZZ and then panicked when I got there. What if he was nothing like the way he sounds? I liked him being my fantasy man, and meeting him might ruin everything. I had to force myself to go inside.

When I went in, the front-desk girl told me that I could go into the studio, but to watch what I said . . . DJ Scotty was on the air.

I took a deep breath and opened the door. . . .

Wow! He was wearing ripped jeans, a black T-shirt, and biker boots. He was tall, with a nice body, and tattoos everywhere. They were all over his muscular arms

and on his chest and neck. He was nothing like I had expected! But he was sexy and had perfect teeth and a great smile.

"Hey . . . you're a hot one," he said in his deep sexy voice. "Come over and let me have a good look at you," he said, as he checked me out and swung the mic toward me.

I walked closer to him and introduced myself on the air.

Scotty took the mic and said he'd be back after a break. He turned down the sound, took off his headphones, and stood up to properly introduce himself to me.

"Might I just add . . . you look fucking amazing. We had about six other girls, and you are the best one by far. Please sit down."

"Oh, I can't stay. Plus, you have a show to do," I said, grinning.

"Don't worry, most of my show is prerecorded. I don't have to be back on air for at least an hour." He pushed some papers off his desk and sat on it. The studio was so small that I was practically standing between his open legs. "Hey, you're that sexy bartender at

Bareys, right? I thought I recognized you," Scotty said, looking me up and down.

I was flattered that he recognized me and knew who I was. That was so cool. The more we talked, the less intimidated I was by him. He was really funny and flirtatious, so of course I flirted back.

We talked a bit and I told him about my obsession with his deep sexy voice. He laughed and told me I was too cute. But letting him know that just made things crazy! He started touching me and flirting heavily now that he knew I had the hots for him.

We'd been talking for about fifteen minutes when he slipped his arm around my hips, pulled me toward him, and started kissing me. It was ballsy of him, and I loved it. I mean: we'd just met! I thought it was the sexiest thing—something I'd never done before—so I just went with it.

I put my hands in his hair and yanked back his head to kiss his neck. He roughly picked me up and sat me on his desk. I weigh only 112 pounds so it was easy for him to toss me around. He then pushed up my miniskirt and pulled my top over my head, and he started sucking on my tits and rubbing my clit. Just the

thought of someone hearing us or walking in made me so hot.

He continued to suck and finger me until I was soaking my panties. Then he smiled, turned on some punk music, and began licking my pussy with long strokes of his tongue. I was really into it. I could have come in just the first few minutes. I'd had so much tension in me for months thinking about him.

Scotty pulled back and unzipped his jeans and pushed them down his legs. Scotty pulled my hips toward him, massaged his dick a little, making it good and hard, and then roughly shoved it inside me. I grabbed the mic above my head for leverage, moaning as I let him have his way with me. I don't think anyone heard us. If they did they didn't say anything.

Scotty banged me hard for a long time, holding tightly to my hips until I could feel he was close to coming. As he was about to come, I slid off him and slipped his dick into my mouth, sucking him hard.

I'm so glad I went down to meet my fantasy man. Scotty and I are going to the concert tonight . . . and together.

I just moved into my sweet New York apartment last month from my home in Florida. It's quite a change, but I'm starting to get used to it. I haven't been here long, but from what I've seen, it's fast-paced and the women here are very sophisticated. I want to meet a girl who likes to play, loves to laugh, and won't go crazy if she shows up to work five minutes late!

There's this girl who works at the bookstore in my building. She's gorgeous, with a soft, innocent look to her. She's tall; I'd say five feet nine inches or so, with long luscious legs that she always pairs with perfect heels. Her hips sway so nicely as she walks, and her bright baby blues see me every morning through the window as I pass by on my way

to work. I know she's seen me walk by for the last month; well, at least I sure have noticed her.

A few days ago, after continuing to see the girl behind the glass, I thought it couldn't hurt to bring her a coffee and introduce myself. Everyone likes coffee, and if she doesn't . . . even better, I'd ask her out to tea!

I paced around the bookstore like a fucking idiot, holding two coffees and wondering if I was about to make an ass out of myself.

Then she walked up to me.

"Can I help you find something in nonfiction?" she asked.

"A non whata?" I stammered. I was stunned; I hadn't seen her coming.

"Nonfiction. You're in the nonfiction section, sir," she replied.

God! I was such an idiot! Then I panicked and lost my train of thought.

"Oh, actually, I wanted to give you this coffee. I see you every morning and noticed how beautiful you are, and I thought it wouldn't hurt to drop this off," I said, hoping she wouldn't walk off thinking I was crazy.

"I'm working, and I don't drink on the job," she said, joking. "But I can drink coffee after work." She smiled.

Thank God, I thought to myself.

"I'm Andrew. I live upstairs. When do you get off?"

"Seven, Andrew. I'm Hannah. I'll see you then," she said, as she walked away looking hot in her long tight pencil skirt and pumps.

As I walked back upstairs I thought to myself that it must be my lucky day. A nice girl like Hannah doesn't usually date guys like me.

When I showed up at seven P.M. she was locking the store's door. She let me inside so I could wait until she finished up.

"Andrew, right?" she asked. "Follow me so no one sees you in the widow," she said, walking toward the back.

I wondered what was going on, but I definitely didn't want to get her into trouble, so I followed her.

"I'm sorry to make you wait, Andrew, but let me close out these cash drawers, then we can be on our way."

Okay . . . I thought to myself. But why didn't she just ask me show up at seven-thirty? It's not like I cared, but why was she still in the middle of closing?

Hannah went behind a counter and started to finish up the paperwork. She kicked off her four-inch heels and unbuttoned several of the buttons on her blouse, showing a fair amount of cleavage. She loosened her hair and pushed up her sleeves. I sat there in silence, thinking this must be a dream.

"Andrew, can you please unzip my skirt?" she asked.

I stood up, walked over to her, and unzipped her skirt. She stepped out of them and was wearing a garter belt and no panties. This must be a dream, I thought. Hannah then turned around, slid her hands behind my head, and put her soft lips against mine. When she opened her mouth and slipped her tongue inside, my dick hardened. I couldn't believe I was making out in the bookstore with Hannah, the girl of my dreams. I picked her up and placed her on the counter. Her shirt hung open, exposing her lacy black bra. I unclasped her bra, and her gorgeous tits fell out. They were beautiful, full, and firm, with thick nipples. I massaged them,

sucking on her nipples, and she wrapped her legs around my waist. All the while I couldn't believe what we were doing. When she started moaning, I got down on my knees and spread her legs wider, then I kissed her inner thighs and made my way slowly toward the triangle between her legs. Her long fit legs smelled like roses, and her body was so soft and supple. My tongue ached to taste her.

Was this really happening?

When I'd kissed and licked my way to her clit, I pushed her thighs even farther apart and slipped her long legs over my shoulders; then I pushed Hannah back on the counter. She was so gorgeous lying there with her hair spread out behind her and her breasts so full and sexy. I then opened her lips and licked her roughly with my tongue until her whole body started to shake with pleasure and she was moaning and rolling her head back and forth. When I reached up and started rubbing her breasts, Heather's breathing became rough and she started to tremble. I knew she was close to coming. I took my other hand and slipped a finger inside her, banging her gently. Heather bucked her hips off the

counter and started coming. I could feel her wetness coating my fingers.

Later Heather said she'd seen me on my way to work for the last few weeks and had wanted to meet me.

I'm seeing her again tomorrow.

Since I'm a 32D, which is practically a specialty size, I don't always find a bra that fits well! But a friend told me to check out Vicki's Lingerie Store, because they carry a lot of specialty sizes.

When I arrived at the shop, they had the most awesome selection of summer lingerie in pinks, yellows, and blues. When I saw this fabulous, cotton candy pink bra-and-panty set, I just about died! It was sheer, with fancy lace ruffles. I'd seen a similar outfit a few months back in a catalogue, and I just had to try it on! Problem was, the bra was a 32C.

I went into the dressing room door to squeeze my petite figure into the pink two-piece. The panties looked just great, but as expected the bra was a bit tight. I rang the dressing room bell for a sales associate.

"Did you need help in there?" the salesgirl asked.

I reached my hand over the top of the dressing room door and handed her the bra.

"Do you have this in a 32D?" I asked hopefully.

"Let me go take a look," she said, taking the bra from my hand.

When she came back, she had bad news. She said the 32C was the largest size they carried in this style.

"If you'd like, I can come in and measure your bust to see if we might have a comparable size. You never know . . . a 34C might work," she said.

Being so down on the fact that the bra wasn't fitting, I said okay. Then I opened the dressing room door so the sales associate could come in and measure me.

When she walked in, I stood there in the pink ruffled panties with my hands covering my breasts. She was adorable, with thick honey-colored hair hanging down her back and bangs cut straight across her forehead. Her golden tan complemented her hazel eyes. She was wearing tight low jeans and a baby T-shirt that barely reached her navel. Her name tag said KELLY.

"Okay, just turn around and let me get this measuring tape around your bust," Kelly said with a smile.

The measuring tape was so cold across my nipples that it made them very hard. The cute salesgirl standing so close behind me just made things worse.

I'm thirty-one and at my sexual peak. Having a sexy twenty-year-old girl touch my body was sending shivers down my spine. I was getting turned on.

When she was finished, I turned to face her.

"Maybe I should just get breast reduction so I won't have such a hard time finding bras," I joked.

"Oh, please . . . I only wish I had a 32D kind of a problem. You look amazing," she said, admiring my breasts. As she looked at them my nipples got harder. I knew Kelly could tell I was turned on. "Can I touch 'em?" she asked.

I'd been hoping she'd ask me that.

I took both of her hands and placed them on my boobs. She smiled and started to caress my tits, weighing them in her hands. She then rubbed her palm over my nipples. When I smiled at her, she stepped closer to me and began to suck on one of my nipples. It felt so good. She was so beautiful, and up close I could see the freckles across her nose. I wanted more.

I pushed her against the wall and hiked her T-shirt

up over her breasts. Then I unzipped her jeans, slipped a finger inside her panties, and rubbed her pussy. She was so soft and definitely shaved. I was getting wetter and wetter as I stroked her clit. Kelly was breathing heavily and rubbing my tits harder. I fingered her and then gave her a long kiss. I could see the goose bumps she was getting. And she kept moaning and grinding her hips against my hand. It was so sexy. I played with her nipples, pinching them and giving them long wet licks. I knew she was close. I kept fingering her until she whispered, "I'm coming." She then came all over my fingers, and her body shook against me. It made my day.

I have to say . . . that was some great customer service!

I'm not a very good swimmer, so this summer I decided to take swimming lessons. Now, I know that you usually take swimming lessons at age four or five, not at twenty-five, but I figured it was better late than never.

When I got to Ranch Park Pool for my first lesson, it felt a bit strange that the lifeguard and I were the only adults there. Even my swimming instructor had to be only fifteen! But the real treat was the lifeguard, Sam. He's so sexy. Muscular and very tanned, he looks just like the ones on TV. Actually, I'd had a crush on Sam since my senior year in high school. But he didn't know it because we had gone to different schools.

I was wearing my new black bikini, and as the lesson went on, I made sure to get Sam's attention by walking in front of

him every time I got out of the pool. I could feel his stares when I walked by. I even did my best to bend over in front of him to get my towel. When the lesson was finished, he walked up to me.

"Hey, don't I know you?" Sam asked. Of course he didn't; that was just his cheesy pickup line, probably used on every chick who swims at the pool.

"Nope, don't think so," I answered. Two could play that game, I thought.

He held out his hand. "I'm Sam. What's your name?"

I smiled and shook his hand. "I'm Ashley."

"Hi, Ashley." Sam smiled. "I see you're learning to swim. Can I buy you a smoothie? I'll give you some tips. I get off in ten minutes. You could change and meet me back here. Whaddaya say?" he finished, with a sexy smile.

Of course I said yes.

I went to the locker room, slipped on a pair of my sexy denim shorts and platform sandals, pulled the band out of my hair, and shook it free.

Ten minutes later, Sam was getting ready for his break as another lifeguard came on duty. He smiled at

me, took my hand, and led me through the employee doors to the showers. He then turned on one of the showers and told me he needed to clean up. As he stepped under the running water, he motioned for me to join him, telling me that I looked sexy wet. Can you believe it?

Being the naughty girl I am, I stepped out of my sandals, pulled off my denim shorts, and got under with him. The water running down his muscular swimmer's body turned me on something fierce! I was getting chills just from watching him take a shower. When I put my head under the water to slick back my hair, Sam leaned toward me and kissed my shoulder. I grabbed his chin and kissed his full lips. I put his hand on my waist and slipped my hand around his and pulled him close. Our wet bodies felt so slick. I could feel his erection through his wet trunks, and our swimsuits were just getting in the way. We were really going at it by now.

Our kissing became more intense as Sam pulled my head back by my hair and gave me deep wet kisses. Sam then slipped a hand inside my bikini bottom and played with my clit, rubbing it just the way I liked. I pressed

my hips against his erection and opened my legs a little wider. Sam slid two fingers inside me and sucked a nipple into his mouth, nibbling on it. Oh, it felt so good, his wet fingers inside me, his hard-on against my thighs, and his tongue on my breasts. I couldn't believe what was happening. I'd had a crush on Sam for years, and here we were with his hand between my legs. I was getting close to coming. When he started stroking my clit, I took a deep breath and tried to hold back my orgasm, but I just couldn't. . . .

I moaned loudly and tensed up, then I came all over Sam's hand. It didn't matter; we were already in the shower. Sam didn't get to come, but . . . he was at work and I was a paying customer.

Maybe next time, Sam.

After having my boss practically chew my ass out all day for not taking the proper inventory, I needed to relax. I would have booked myself at the nearest spa, but it was getting a bit late. I'd probably have a better time at home in my own bed.

I rushed home, poured myself a glass of red wine, then made my way upstairs to run a hot bath. A relaxing bubble bath with coconut-scented candles seemed like just what I needed.

I stood in front of the bathroom mirror and piled my long hair on top of my head, then I stepped out of my itchy work clothes. First I pulled my navy tank top over my head and slipped off my knee-length skirt. My tight bra was killing me, and I was thrilled to unsnap it and let my breasts fall free. Having to wear heels every day is very tiring, and I was look-

ing forward to a long soak. When I was undressed, I slipped my aching body into the hot bubble bath.

I lay there trying hard to relax. But thinking of what I had gone through all day made it very hard. I reached over and turned on some soft tunes and started massaging my body. I slowly started rubbing my tense neck and shoulders, making my way up to my head. I was sore all over. Even my breasts seemed tender as I rubbed them gently, covering the nipples in the bath bubbles.

As I rubbed my breasts I could feel my nipples harden, and a tingling started between my legs. I was finally starting to relax. I reached down between my thighs, found my clit, and started caressing myself. Hmm . . . I closed my eyes and let my head fall back against the tub as my fingers continued to tease my body.

I was turning myself on and wanted to come so badly. An orgasm would help me to relax and allow me to sleep in peace.

I turned on the faucet and slid my body down the tub to allow the warm running water to massage my clit. I rocked my body back and forth to angle myself

just right. The warm water raced down my body, turning me on. I moaned and moaned, wanting to feel my thick cum slide down my thighs with the running water. When the water did its job, I felt such a relief and finally relaxed. I spent a few more moments in the tub gathering my thoughts. But all I could think was . . . I should do this more often.

This past Memorial Day weekend I couldn't wait to go camping at the lake. It was going to be *so* much fun. All the girls were going, and we'd decided there'd be no boys on the trip.

I packed up my Jeep with my bikinis, flashlights, and booze. You know . . . the necessities. All I had to do then was pick up my crew of divas, and we'd be on our way. I was single, but my girlfriends rarely got away from their boyfriends for an entire weekend. . . . So this trip was a big deal.

When we got to the campsite, we found the best location. Beautiful blue waters, green trees, and rocks to lie on. It was just perfect. Well, almost perfect. A group of guys pulled up to the campsite next to us. And they were definitely there to party.

As day turned into night, their party grew louder. Don't get me wrong, we can definitely get rowdy, but these guys were acting as if they owned the lake. I grabbed my friend Johnna and told her that we were gonna set those loud guys straight. I actually didn't care *that* much about the noise, but I thought our trip might be more fun if we got to meet some hot strangers. Johnna was totally buzzed, but she agreed and grabbed her drink, and we were on our way.

"Hi, I'm Lindsay, and this is my friend Johnna. We're camping just right over there from you guys, and I was hoping that maybe you could turn it down a bit," I said, as I pointed to our campsite.

Boy, was I right! It was Hottie Central over there. There must have been at least nine or ten guys in the camp, and they were all so nice and polite. They apologized for the loud noise and any inconveniences, and a few of them even asked if they could come back with us to meet the other girls. Of course Johnna and I were all over that idea.

I guess the girls were also hoping we'd bring a few guys back with us, because when we returned to our

tent, their hair and makeup looked pretty excellent for having been camping all day.

Everyone got along well, and I was happy to have brought the guys over. We continued to drink and have a great time. I especially got along with Kyle. *Wow!* What a great guy. He was the whole package: good-looking, a great bod, smart, and funny.

It started to get colder as the night went on. But I didn't really complain 'cause I didn't want Kyle to leave. So I suggested he spend a little time with me in my Jeep instead of the monster-size tent my girl-friends and I were sharing. He agreed without hesitation.

We sat up front and I fiddled with my new satellite radio as he rubbed my thigh. I knew from the first second I saw Kyle that I had to have him. I leaned in to kiss him on his lips. Hmm . . . His lips were so full and soft. It was just a taste of what was to come. I grabbed onto the Jeep's roll bar and pulled myself over Kyle and straddled him. I started kissing his neck and rubbing my tight-jean-covered pussy against his thighs. He really seemed to be enjoying himself. He grabbed my ass

cheeks and ground me down on his hard package. I started to get wet and very hot for him.

He untied my bikini top and buried his face in my chest as he continued to grind his hips up into me. We unzipped each other's jeans and wiggled them down our bodies. He was nice and big, just my type. I once again grabbed onto my Jeep roll bar and lifted up, allowing Kyle to rub the head of his package on my wet puss. Mmm, I was moaning even before he'd shoved himself in me. I bounced myself up and down by holding on to the bar. It was very handy. We were going so fast, my breasts were bouncing in his face. My arms were getting tired, and just when I thought I couldn't take it anymore, Kyle moaned loudly, pulled out, and came all over my stomach.

This was by far the sexiest trip I've ever been on. Hopefully the shaking Jeep didn't give away that we were up to something.

I had invited over a few friends to play poker, and I was hoping April Hill would show up, too. It was rumored that she had it for me. She was the hottest girl at my university. To say the least, she looks like a model.

Every time I look into her hazel eyes, her beauty mesmerizes me.

I was stoked when my whole crew showed up. But when April walked in with a few unexpected hotties . . . I got really excited. Who wouldn't want four hot chicks at a poker party? I served my lovely guests with a few drinks while Howard dealt the cards. It seemed as if April and her friends were having a really great time. They were laughing and flirting quite a bit.

After a few crappy hands and several drinks later, April suggested strip poker.

"Hey, Chad, how about a few hands of strip poker," she said to me as she sipped her drink.

Did she think I was gonna say no?

"That's a great idea," I said with a smile. "Standard rules apply to everyone, and no cheating." I didn't want anyone trying to get out of it if they lost. We were all in this together now.

Right around the third hand, I started losing big-time. I was almost naked! This was not the way I had expected it to turn out. I knew I'd be hearing about this from my friends for a very long time.

Just when I thought I was going to have to show my ass, April folded then came and sat next to me. After losing her top and jeans, she didn't want to play anymore. Go figure! But she sure made me feel a whole lot better for being almost naked. After curling up next to me, she reached under my boxer briefs and started rubbing my balls under the table. Oh, my God . . . I was in heaven! I didn't want anyone to see, but it was hard to keep my eyes from rolling around in my head with pleasure. I stood up and asked April to help me in the kitchen getting drinks for everyone.

As soon as we walked through the swinging kitchen door, we started making out.

I caressed her gorgeous breasts through her lace bra. When she leaned back against the kitchen counter, I started kissing her—from her full tits with their light nipples to her sexy triangle. Her lightly tanned skin felt soft, like silk, and she smelled like powder. I was so turned on. I lifted her up onto the counter, pulled off her panties, and started licking her pussy. She was so wet and tasted so sweet. April arched her back and started moaning as I roughly licked her clit and slid my tongue in and out of her pussy, getting her juices all over my face. My dick was hard for her. I wanted to make her come so badly. I pulled myself out of my boxers and slid my dick inside April. Her pussy was already really wet.

April started moaning like crazy, pushing her hips up against me, so I gave it to her harder and harder. Her head started banging the cupboard doors, and her moans got even louder. I was worried that someone might come in, so I muffled her mouth with my hand and fucked her really hard, squeezing her nipples until

her body tightened and she came, moaning loudly. Feeling her body shake against me from her orgasm made me come only seconds after she did. It was one of the best sexual experiences I've ever had. I will always remember my "poke-her" night with April Hill.

I'm a mathematics professor at a major university out here in Ohio. Rumor has it that I'm an easy A if you can get on my good side; I love my job, and I take it very seriously. No hanky-panky from me. I'm a married man in my forties. What interest would I have in the eighteen-year-old freshmen girls I teach?

But then Mandy came along. It's easy to see that Mandy is spoiled, and very naughty. She wears the tiniest outfits to school, and she gets a lot of male attention. She works her gorgeous brown eyes, long blond hair, and freckles to her advantage. I hardly ever see her wear makeup. Of course, beauty like hers doesn't need it. But when she becomes a major distraction in my math class, I have to discipline her.

Last week I had Mandy stay after class to discuss her attire. When I told her that I thought her outfits were inappropriate, she started to cry, saying that all the girls her age dress this way and that I was picking on her. I had to stay strong and get my point across. But at the same time, I wondered if I *was* picking on her. It was true: many of the girls wore skimpy outfits to class. But Mandy's beauty coupled with her tiny outfits caused more of a stir. I must be a total sucker because Mandy had me questioning my intentions toward her and feeling bad about talking to her.

She was wearing one of the smallest skirts I've ever seen in my life. After we'd finished talking, she sat down on my roller chair, lifted her knees to her chest and continued to cry, her arms propped on her knees. I could see between her legs. Her baby blue and yellow thong barely covered anything. I couldn't believe she was sitting like that in front of me. I couldn't even get the words out of my mouth because I was starting to get hard. Talk about an awkward situation.

I quickly sat on the edge of my desk, crossed my legs, and put the folder I was holding over my lap to cover my hard-on. She looked up at me with her big

brown eyes, a tear or two running down her face, and asked to be excused. Of course I said yes.

She stood up and adjusted her skirt to cover herself. She was walking toward the classroom door when she dropped her book. Then she did the damndest thing: she looked me in the eyes, crossed her ankles, and bent *all the way* over to pick up her book. That was one amazing view. She has the nicest, tightest ass I had ever seen. I couldn't wait for her to leave so I could lock the door and jerk off thinking about her. She really turned me on. I don't even care about her clothes anymore. She can wear whatever she wants.

My husband, Shaun, is away all this week on business. As usual, I'm left at home bored and lonely. I always miss him so much. We've just moved here and have a large and beautiful home. But I don't know many people yet, so I'm often by myself when he's away. So I've gotten into the habit of spending time online in chat rooms. It's not so bad. I've actually met a few really cool people on the Web. Not in person . . . Shaun would be so mad! Shoot, he'd be mad if he knew I was spending so much time on the computer in general. He's never gotten into the online chat thing, so he doesn't really understand.

On a typical night before bed, I take a shower then sit at my desk in my robe, lonely, and I surf the Internet wishing Shaun were with me. But at least I have the computer, and

one night earlier this week I met Anissa, a really great girl from Sweden. I love to meet other people from around the world. We met each other in a "Sharing Baking Recipes" chat room. Anissa gave me a wonderful recipe for raspberry chocolate-chip cookies.

Anissa seemed sweet and down to earth, and we had a lot in common. We were both married, loved green tea, and are both twenty-five years old. The more we "talked," the more we found we had in common. We must have been online with each other for hours. When I told Anissa that Shaun and I own a tanning salon, she told me that she sunbathed in the nude to avoid tan lines. As we talked Anissa sent me a picture of herself naked on the beach. Boy, was she gorgeous! She's tall with long white-blond hair, green eyes, and pouty lips. She was sitting in a beach chair with her long tanned legs stretched out in front of her. Her breasts were gorgeous, full and tanned, with slightly darker nipples. Anissa was one of those lucky women, tall, thin, and also busty. She was smiling into the camera, and her look was a little naughty. I almost couldn't type back; I just kept staring at her picture.

When Anissa typed that she wanted to see a picture

of me on the beach, my heart started pounding. I don't know why just the idea of our looking at each other's body while we "chatted" gave me a tingling between my thighs. Gosh, I wished Shaun were here. I couldn't believe I was getting horny in a baking chat room. But the picture of Anissa naked on the beach made me start to think very naughty thoughts about my new friend.

I found a picture that Shaun had taken of me one weekend when we'd gone camping on the beach. We'd just made love, and Shaun had posed me naked on my sleeping bag, with my long hair tousled around my breasts. I have my hands up behind my head, and one leg is crossed over the other, just barely giving a glimpse of my pussy, which was still wet from our lovemaking. My eyes look sleepy, and I have a slight smile on my lips. Looking at the picture, it's easy to figure out that I'd just had sex.

Before I changed my mind I sent the picture to Anissa. A moment later she typed back that I was very beautiful and that my husband was a very lucky man. She then wrote that my picture had made her horny and that her husband wasn't due home for a few hours.

I just stared at the words. I was shocked but also

turned on. I wrote that I thought she had a beautiful body, too. As I looked at her picture I could feel myself getting warmer as my blood raced through my body. I missed Shaun and was frustrated. I was getting very hot. I rubbed my breasts through the thin silk of my robe. My nipples were so hard. I pinched one between my fingers and felt myself getting even wetter. I untied the sash of my robe and slipped a finger between my legs. I couldn't believe how wet I was.

I pushed back in my chair and put my legs up on the desk on either side of the computer; then I opened the robe and started touching my breasts. I licked two fingers and rubbed them over my clit, slowly at first, then faster and faster. I pinched my nipples with the other hand and pulled on them as they hardened. I could feel myself getting close to coming. I slipped two fingers inside and started fucking myself slowly and deeply. The whole time I had my eyes on Anissa's picture. She was so hot; her skin was tanned a warm caramel and her hair looked white against it. Her breasts were gorgeous, and I imagined they were her fingers deep inside me. The image of Anissa naked on her knees finger-fucking me

made me come so hard, my body was jerking in the chair as I soaked my fingers. Oh, it felt so good.

When I was able to look up again, I saw Anissa had typed that she would keep my picture private and that whenever we chatted she'd open it and look at me. She typed that she wanted to stay in touch, and maybe one day we could meet.

I typed that I'd keep her picture private, too, and that she should stay in touch. I then thanked her for her recipes and logged off.

I rushed to the bathroom, stepped out of my robe, and got into a shower to cool myself off. Boy, did Shaun have a treat in store when he got home.

My boyfriend, Tyler, seems to be going through an exotic dancer phase. Sometimes I feel like I can't really compete. I mean, those girls are professionals and get paid to be sexy. I'm just a blond southern girl from a small town in Georgia. I would never ask Tyler not to go to the clubs. In fact, sometimes he's even hotter for me when he gets home from a few hours at a club with his friends. But I want to plan something special for him so he doesn't think I'm a total prude.

Tonight when he comes home I'll be wearing a skintight black corset, with a lacy thong and sheer thigh-highs. I'll be in the kitchen making lasagna, his favorite dish. I've never dressed like this before. But tonight, Tyler's in for a treat.

He's just going to love it. The corset will make my breasts look even bigger, and my legs are long and sexy. I'll style my long hair to be curly like a pinup, and my stilettos will make me almost as tall as Tyler.

When Tyler opened the front door, he walked right into the kitchen, sniffing at the scent of the lasagna. Taking one look at me, he put his hands around my waist and said, "Wow, babe. What is this? You look amazing."

That was exactly what I wanted to hear. I turned around and bent over the stove so he could get a good look at me as I stuck my finger in the marinara sauce, then licked it off slowly. The bulge against my ass told me that he was getting turned on. He couldn't keep his hands off me. I expected it, but it was a little over-whelming. I was completed turned on by Tyler wanting me so much. I knew the exotic dancers were completely forgotten and he was thinking only about me. I turned off the stove and took his arm to lead him up-stairs to the bedroom for some playtime.

• • •

Tyler hardly ever goes to the clubs with his buddies since that night. I'm now more open with him, and I know I'm the only girl he thinks about. I'm putting together a new outfit for tonight, but this time our meeting will take place in the garage.

In Europe, soccer is a very popular sport, except there it's called football. I can't mention his name, but last Wednesday night I had the most erotic encounter with a professional football player. He's huge . . . and he's big in Europe, too.

He's about six feet six, with dark blond hair and inviting blue eyes. His mouth is shaped in a perfect bow, and his sexy height and muscular build are enough to turn any woman on. What made me go really wild were his deep voice and his accent. I got chills every time he said my name, Ava.

I met my famous stud at one of the hottest clubs in Dallas. This guy could have had any girl in the place, probably in the whole city, if he wanted, but he wanted me and pursued me all evening. I loved every minute of it. Maybe it was my

silky black hair and crystal blue eyes that made him want me. I'm not sure, but whatever it was he was definitely interested.

After following me around the club for half an hour, he came over and introduced himself. As if he had to! He bought me a drink and we flirted for a bit before he led me over to the roped-off VIP area of the club. It was so beautiful in there. The crystal chandeliers gave the room a nice warm glow, and the low-slung couches and glass tables with their little candles added to the hip vibe. We stood at the bar and talked a little, getting closer and closer to each other with every passing minute. Before long we were seriously making out, pressing our bodies tightly against each other.

I've never been so attracted to someone before. Neither of us could contain ourselves. As we embraced he slipped his leg between my thighs and pressed his hips against mine. When he slipped his big hands around my waist to cup my ass, I squirmed in pleasure. I was so turned on. I could feel my body heating up. He then slipped one rough hand into my low-cut top and grasped one of my breasts. My nipples hardened from

shock and desire. I could feel the warmth between my legs as he caressed my nipple.

I grabbed him by the waist and held him even tighter. When I leaned back against the bar, he came closer and kissed my neck, making his way to nibble on my ear. He pulled back and easily lifted my petite body up onto the bar; then he buried his face between my breasts. I could feel his hard dick through my tight jeans. It was easily a good eight or nine inches long. He made his way back to my lips and kissed me gently, whispering against my lips that he wanted to get to know me better. He sounded sincere, and I definitely wanted to get to know him better. This couldn't be happening, I thought; he was a *huge* star. I was overwhelmed and extremely turned on. Soon he worked his lips back down to my cleavage. I wrapped my legs tightly around him, and we continued to get hot and heavy until we heard "last call." We didn't want to stop, but we remembered we could go only so far in public. He lifted me off the bar and led me by the hand out to his car to continue our time together in private.

It's amazing what you can get away with in the VIP when you're famous. "Football" is my new favorite sport.

Every year I vacation in West Hollywood and stay in my favorite trendy hotel that has gorgeous views of L.A.. I was there most recently in this sweet-ass room with a balcony that overlooked Sunset Boulevard. The views were to die for!

It was Friday night, and most of young Hollywood was getting ready for a night out on the town, so I wanted to go to a pretty happenin' hot spot. I called my good friend Mike to see what was going on around town. He's the best club promoter out there. He would know what's up.

Mike agreed to pick me up and take me to a few clubs. Mike and I had dated for several months in the past, but I hadn't seen him in over a year. He's six feet three inches, with a muscular body, dark hair, and Bambi brown eyes. He was

quite the ladies' man, and whenever we went out, he always got a lot of attention. I think it was his ruggedness. I was glad to see him, and he seemed pretty excited to see me, too.

When we got to the club, girls swarmed all over Mike and even bought him drinks. I was a bit jealous, but I knew his interest had to be in me. After all, I'm told I look as good as the rich and famous.

After a few hours we left the club. I'd wanted to stay longer, but I was so jet-lagged. Mike drove me back and walked me up to my room. I invited him in for a drink and to catch up.

I'd really missed Mike and was grateful to spend time with him. We walked outside to my hotel balcony and held hands as we looked at the glittering city lights and the sparkling stars.

We talked about old times and smoked a few cigarettes before our love connection got too intense to handle. The screwdrivers were kicking in, and the moonlight shining in his eyes made things truly romantic.

Mike put his hands on my shoulders and pushed me toward the corner of the balcony, then moved in for a

kiss. It was hot. I grabbed him by the waist and pulled him closer, and then I reached down his low-rider jeans and grabbed his hard cock.

I gave him a tease of a hand job then slid my back down the balcony wall and got down on my knees so I could put his huge dick in my mouth.

"Mmm . . . you taste so good, Mike," I said as licked his cock and played with his balls.

All I can remember his saying is, "Oh, fuck yeah . . ."

I sucked his throbbing cock for so long my mouth was getting dryer and dryer.

"Oh, yeah . . . Fuck my mouth," I moaned. "I love it when you fuck my mouth!"

He loved my dirty talk and told me he was going to come down my throat.

I gagged more on his cock and continued stroking the lower part with my hand. He pushed my head up and down to get what he wanted and then shouted, "I'm coming," as he busted a nut all down my throat and even my chin.

Mike not only looked good, he also tasted good. I was looking forward to our next encounter.

Until next time . . . Mike.

I've wanted a sports car for some time now. I've done plenty of research online and know quite a bit about pricing and horsepower. I figured by now I knew enough to get by in a conversation with a salesman at the local dealership. So last Friday, after making a few more quick notes, I headed to the car lot to make my final decision. . . . It turned into an experience I'll never forget.

When someone who looks like me pulls up to a sports dealership, there's always at least three salesmen ready to fight for the privilege of waiting on me. I'm twenty-nine, with long sun-bleached hair and sexy tanned legs. I'm told my legs are my best feature, so I love to show them off. I guess I like the attention; if I didn't, I suppose I'd wear baggy sweatpants.

A moment after I got out of my car, a salesman walked up to me. "Hi, I'm Aaron. Can I help you find something special or in particular?" he asked.

I stood there and looked at him, trying to figure him out. He was about twenty-seven or twenty-eight, blue-green eyes, and stood about five feet nine inches tall. If I'd had my usual high heels on, we'd have been the same height! I'm usually attracted to tall men, but Aaron was cute in his own way.

I explained to him that I was looking for a white convertible with at least three hundred horsepower and that I needed to test-drive it as well.

Aaron walked me over to the white convertible sports car of my dreams, gave me a big smile, opened the driver's door, and said, "Step in." I was *so* excited. This car was way hotter than my old car, which I seem to scratch in the same place at every gas pump.

I stepped into the driver's seat, and Aaron got in the other side. The minute we left the dealership, he started putting some serious moves on me. First, he complimented me on the color of my eyes, then on my hair, my chest, and my legs. He seemed to be working his way down my body. He wouldn't let up. Just because

I'm wearing a short sundress doesn't mean I'm asking for a date . . . Jeez!

As I continued to test-drive my dream car I was getting more hot and excited for it. The wind in my hair, the revving as I shifted gears, the rumbling of the engine vibrating my thighs were turning me on.

In my cutest voice I asked Aaron what the car's sticker price was, and whether this model is much cheaper used. He told me that obviously used cars are significantly less expensive than new cars, but that this car was new.

I had to have this car . . . but I had to get a great deal, so I played my cute-blonde act for the next mile and then placed his hand on my upper thigh. I could tell he really liked that. He must have felt pretty comfortable because his hand just kept sliding farther up my thigh.

I pulled over so Aaron could drive. "I want to go really fast, but I'm scared to drive that fast myself," I told him.

When we got out of the car to switch seats, I noticed Aaron had a total hard-on. It was kind of flattering, and it turned me on even more.

When he started driving, I kept yelling, "Faster,

faster, go faster!" He did just that. Oh, God, it was so sexy to be moving so fast down the highway. I was so hot. I reached up my dress and started playing with myself, pushing my skirt up so Aaron would have a good view. The wind between my legs was cooling me down even as what I was doing with my fingers was heating me up. It was so hot to be jerking off in a car moving fast on the open road. I leaned even farther back in the seat and put my feet up on the dash. Poor Aaron had to keep both hands on the wheel.

With one hand I massaged my breasts and with the other I stroked my clit, making myself slick. I was sure there'd be a mess on the seat when I was done, but I didn't care. When I felt myself getting close to coming, I slipped a finger deep inside me and started fingering myself, moving my finger in and out. I was so close to coming; the air rushing around between my legs and blowing my hair around me was so erotic. When Aaron gunned the engine and we surged forward, I came hard all over the sand-colored leather seats.

Of course I bought the car, and the great news is that the car was definitely *used!* You wouldn't believe the great deal I got!